The Duke and the Dalesman's Daughter

Anne Harlowe

Published by EKP, 2019.

This is a work of fiction. Similarities to real people, places, or events are entirely coincidental.

THE DUKE AND THE DALESMAN'S DAUGHTER

First edition. March 21, 2019.

Copyright © 2019 Anne Harlowe.

ISBN: 979-8224805617

Written by Anne Harlowe.

Table of Contents

To my fellow students at Leeds University, with whom I studied Jane Austen, my introduction to Regency Romance, and to one student in particular, who introduced me to raunch.

The Romeo of the Road

"We won't get there until past two now," complained Lord Collingham, who had just pressed the button of his repeater, which told him that it was midnight.

He pulled back the curtain of the window to try to see where they were, but it was as black outside as inside. All he could make out was the silhouette of trees against a moonlight-silvered sky.

"At least we are not missing anything," said his good wife, "for the duke's house party does not begin until tomorrow."

"Then we should have set off in first thing tomorrow morning. It's never a good idea to travel by night."

"If we had done that we should have arrived late for the reception. It is a good nine hours from Grantham to Dale Hall, and I should look a fright after such a long journey!"

Lord Collingham did his best to control his irritation. He had only himself to blame, after all. Maria had fussed about packing her trunk, about which gowns to take, and which to leave behind, changed her mind, told her maid to take everything out, then made a new selection. By the time she was ready, it had gone six o'clock, but she had insisted that it was better to make a start that evening so that she could have the next morning to prepare herself for the reception.

"Anyway, what is wrong with travelling at night? There are good turnpike roads all the way, and there is hardly any traffic."

"We must turn off at Wetherby, and the roads are bad. It will be hard for John to see his way."

Lord Collingham looked again out of the window.

"Where are we, my dear?"

"There's dense woodland on either side, so we must be passing through Bramham Woods. We will change horses at Wetherby and take some refreshment."

The thought of a glass of claret cheered him considerably, and he settled back to try to sleep. His good lady was not tired, however, and continued to engage him in conversation.

"Is this where Robin Hood robbed the rich and gave to the poor?"

"No, we passed that hours ago. Do you remember? I mentioned Robin Hood's Well."

"Yes."

"But there *is* a link with Wetherby. There was a Robert of Wetherby who was accused of being Robin Hood."

Lady Collingham gave a pleasant shudder, very much like the ones she gave when reading gothic novels. "Thank God those days are gone!"

Just then, the carriage came to a halt.

"We can't be in Wetherby already!" exclaimed her husband, letting down the window by the leather strap.

The scene outside was the same: black silhouettes of huge oak trees against the background of a moonlight sky.

"What is it John?" he called.

There was no answer, just a whimpering sound from Betsy, his lady's maid, and the heavy breathing of the tired horses. Then John said, in a warning voice, "It's a 'old up, sir."

Collingham jumped out of the carriage to see for himself, and sure enough, on the road ahead, silhouetted against the moonlight, were two figures on horseback pointing pistols at them.

"Your money or your life!" said one, in a voice muffled by the scarf around his face.

"What is it?" said Maria, peering out of the doorway.

"Nothing, my dear. Shut the door and stay inside."

"Is it a highwayman?" she said, in a tremulous voice.

Collingham didn't answer. He gently pushed her back into the carriage and shut the door. This was man's work, and though he was ill prepared, he would deal with it as best as he could. He cursed himself for not bringing his pistols. His father had always travelled with pistols, but then, the roads were much more dangerous in his day. In these days of turnpike roads, light, fast carriages, and horse patrols to protect against highwaymen, such a precaution had seemed unnecessary.

The lead highwayman dismounted, walked up to Collingham, pointed his pistol in his face and said, "Put your money and your valuables in this sack. Quickly now, and no tricks, or somebody might get hurt."

The light from the carriage lamp cast a yellow gleam over his face. He was wearing a beaver hat with the brim pulled low, a mask over his eyes, and the lower part of his face was hidden by a voluminous scarf.

"Sir," said Collingham in his sternest voice. "This is an outrage! Give me a pistol and let us fight it out fair and square."

The highwayman laughed.

"But I am not fair and square or I wouldn't be a highwayman."

His voice was slightly muffled by the scarf, but it was clearly that of a cultured and well-educated man. Whoever he was, he was no common thug.

"I will ask you one more time to choose between the alternatives I have put before you: your money or your life. For myself, I am a gentleman, and abhor violence. But Riff Raff, here, has been brought up in a hard school."

At this point, Riff Raff rode closer to the carriage, and said in a rough Dalesman's brogue, "Yer money or yer life!" and fired one of his pistols to underline the point.

The women screamed, the horses bucked, and John called out, "Easy nah!" to settle them down.

Collingham, realising that there was nothing he could do, decided that he would at least try to keep his dignity, and if he could, get away without losing everything.

"Very well, here is my purse."

The gentleman highwayman put it into his pocket without looking to see how much it contained, and the rough highwayman said, "An' the rest! What's in that trunk?"

"My lady's gowns."

He pointed his pistol at Lane, Lord Collingham's manservant.

"Open it!"

"Belay that!" snapped the gentleman highwayman, countermanding the order. "Open that portmantle instead."

Lane did as he was told, but found only clothing.

"Very well, we'll look inside. Everybody out!"

'Everybody' was just Lady Collingham.

As soon as she opened the door, the gentleman highwayman stuck his pistol in his belt and put out his hand to help her. Riff Raff drew another pistol and covered them all.

"Have no fear, my lady. The Romeo of the Road – for that is what they call me – never disobliges a lady. Indeed," he added, with a touch of gallantry, "when they are as beautiful as you are, he goes out of his way to oblige them."

His words were more than flattery, for Lady Collingham, at thirty-three (though she never admitted to more than twenty-eight) was at the height of her beauty. The two children she had borne so far had done nothing to spoil her perfect hourglass figure, and if childbirth had added something to her waist, it had added even more to her bosom to compensate; not that much could be seen of her shape through her voluminous travelling cloak.

"Then let us go," she said, somewhat reassured by the highwayman's gentlemanly treatment, but still trembling

"That I cannot do, ma'am," said the Romeo of the Road, "because Riff Raff, here, will demand his share. So, if you will excuse me, I will search your carriage."

He stepped inside the carriage and in no time at all found the strongbox which was hidden beneath a seat.

"Pass me the key, sir, if you will."

Collingham shook his head, so without further ado, the Romeo of the Road drew his pistol and shot at the lock. Then he opened the lid and found a veritable heap of gold sovereigns.

"Aha!" he said. "Riff Raff will be well pleased with this!"

Lady Collingham, looking into the carriage, said under her breath to her husband, "What is all that money for?"

Lord Collingham said nothing.

"You brought it for the races, I think."

They had been invited to Dale Hall for Wetherby Race Week, and part of that involved visiting the races and enjoying a little flutter on their favourites. However, a hundred gold sovereigns was more than a little flutter. An argument between man and wife was about to begin. It is wonderful how such arguments can take place in the most inappropriate of places; at a dinner party, at the theatre, in church – or even while being robbed!

Perhaps the Romeo of the Road wanted to prevent this, or perhaps it was part of the routine that gave him his nickname, but he said, "My lady, if you will do me the honour of a cotillion and a kiss, I will spare your lord half his hoard."

"A cotillion, here?" she said, much surprised.

The Romeo of the Road made a bow and said, "I grant you that a cotillion is best danced with a four, but we will not want for music – Riff Raff!"

Riff Raff, who was apparently well used to this proceeding, put away a pistol and took out a tabor. A tabor is a small flute which is well suited to this purpose because it can be played with one hand (leaving the other free to tote a pistol).

"Now, my lady, take off that cloak, and we will begin."

She took off the cloak, revealing her well-formed figure under her clinging walking dress. He took her hand, and led her a little way from the carriage. Riff Raff started to play, and the couple started to dance, elegant shadows in the moonlight.

Lord Collingham looked on in disbelief. Was this a hold-up or a game of charades? What did this highwayman want that he risked his life dallying with a woman, when those pistol shots might already have alerted the authorities?

At the end of the dance, Collingham saw the Romeo of the Road lean close to his wife and whisper something into her ear. She gave a light laugh and shook her head. After that, he claimed his kiss – and it was more than a mere peck. It seemed to go on for a long time, and Lady Collingham seemed to be enjoying it. At last, Collingham could bear it no longer and said, "Sir, I protest!"

"Shut thy gob!" growled Riff Raff. "'Ee's paid heavily fer it, so let 'im 'ave 'is dues!"

But the kiss ended at that moment, and Riff Raff was instructed to count the sovereigns (it being beneath a gentleman to grub with money).

"A 'undred!" announced Riff Raff after a while.

"Very well, put fifty back. No, make it fifty-one to pay for the repair of the strong box. Well, sir, you will have your stake for the races, and if you will take my advice, you will put it all on Pretty Polly on Lady's Day. She is an outsider, I know, but I have it on good authority that she will turn a few heads."

Then he made his bow and gave some instructions to Riff Raff about freeing the horses from their traces and shooing them so that they could not be pursued. When this was done, they mounted their horses, and galloped into the night.

Lord Collingham gave a sigh of relief. It was over and nobody had been hurt – and it could have been much worse. True, he was forty-nine guineas the worse for the experience, but his wife's jewellery was untouched, he still had his gold repeater, and he had enough money to enjoy a flutter at the races.

He went to get his wife, who was where the Romeo of the Road had left her, swaying around in a sort of partnerless Cotillion, and clearly in a state of shock. He gave her a hug to reassure her, then called for Betsy to bring the smelling salts. After inhaling a dose that would wake the dead, she seemed to come to her senses and murmured the words: "I thought he was going to ravish me!"

"I would have stopped him!" said Collingham, indignantly.

"Oh, my love!" said Lady Collingham with a sob. "You would have tried, and then that Riff Raff would have shot you!"

It was true. If the Romeo of the Road had attempted rape, his honour would have demanded that he tried to stop him – but it would have been certain death. He shuddered at the thought, and took a sniff of the smelling salts himself. My, but it was sharp! It brought him back to reality, and the realization that, in the common saying, a miss is as good as a mile. The important thing now was to pick up the pieces.

"John, go and see if you can find the horses. Take Lane with you."

Then he turned to his wife. "Come, my love. Make yourself comfortable in the carriage. Here is your cloak. Lay down and try to sleep."

It was a good hour before John returned with just two horses.

"We found this one grazing at the side of the road, and I rode him for a while, then we found the other. I reckon the other two have made their way home to the last stage."

The two horses were harnessed to the carriage, and they resumed their journey at a slower pace, arriving at the Swan and Talbot in Wetherby at three in the morning. Lord Collingham tried to persuade his wife to spend the rest of the night there, but she said she could not rest until they had reached Dale Hall. So they took refreshment while a new team was harnessed to the carriage, and continued their journey half an hour later.

The Major Fights a Duel

For once in his life, Major Cawthorpe questioned what he was doing. The clock had just struck one, and he was putting on his dressing gown with the intention of creeping secretly to Lady Linton's boudoir. It was not that he had not done it before, he had – many times, but not under the roof of his mistress's lord and master, and certainly not in her bed. It was the stuff that dishonour was made of – and the major valued his honour more than his life. Oh, he could fight a duel, and had done so on two previous occasions. The fight didn't bother him. After all, he was a crack shot, and was sure to down his man – it was the odium that followed that he did not care for. That last affair had been straightforward enough. A junior officer, a cornet, had accused him of cheating at cards. They had fought a duel, the cornet had been wounded, and honour was upheld, but even then, many had criticised him for fighting such a callow youth. The worst part about it was that he really had been cheating. He had been losing heavily, and was trying to make it up. Indeed, he had been losing for a long time, and the sum total of his debts did not bear thinking about. Everybody in the mess knew about his debts and most of them believed the cornet's version of the incident. It was lucky, then, that the ball had lodged in his shoulder. If he had killed him, the incident would have snowballed out of all proportions, and he would have been cashiered. But to fight a man who was defending his wife's honour was unthinkable. No matter what the outcome, it was a form of dishonour – especially if the deed had been done in the marital bed – especially if her spouse was away on business for the public good. For that was the situation in this case. Lord Linton, the Duke of Wharfedale, was attending the Assizes at York, and was not expected back until the following afternoon. However, it was too late to back out now. His fair enemy, the Duchess of Wharfedale, had challenged him to a different kind of duel, and, as a man of honour, he couldn't back out now.

He peeped out of the door and looked up and down the Long Gallery. The Long Gallery was at right angles to the Great Staircase and led to five master rooms to the west and another five to the east. The duchess had placed him as close to her room as she dared, in the first room to the west (hers was the fourth). The gallery was black as night, lit only by a dim gleam of moonlight which filtered through the high casement at the end of the gallery. This was the major's first test, for all the doors looked the same, and were not numbered (after all, it was a home, not a hotel). He groped along in the darkness and managed to stub his toe on a piece of furniture – a Jacobean sideboard with huge, bulging legs, made of oak so dark that it was almost invisible. He stifled a curse, felt for the wall, hoping to find the next door, and almost knocked over a bust of Charles II – that is to say, he thought it might be Charles II because of the ornate wig, though it was too dark to read the inscription. He found the next door, and carried on. As he got nearer to the end of the gallery it became a little easier to see, and he could make out the portraits on the walls. Just before the fourth door was a full length portrait of the fourth Duke of Wharfedale (the present Duke's father). He stood in a commanding posture dressed in the style of the previous generation: a powdered wig, a long coat without cutaways, knee-breeches, stockings and buckled shoes. The expression was stern, as befitted a man with such wide-ranging obligations, a man who, like the present duke, had more authority in his Yorkshire domains than the king himself had in England. And as the pale moonlight lit those stern features, it seemed he was asserting his familial authority and frowning at the illicit act that the major was contemplating. It was only an effect of the light, but it was enough to make him feel uncomfortable.

"Four!" he said to himself. Then, taking a deep breath in case he had missed a door, he turned the handle and went into the room. The duchess had told him that he would find himself in the sitting room between the Duke's private quarters and her own, and that he was to go straight forward until he came to another door.

The major picked his way gingerly, for there was no light at all in here, and the last thing he wanted to do was to trip up and wake the household by the noise of his fall. He made it safely to the next door, however, and turned the handle cautiously. After all, if it were the wrong room, he might happen upon the dowager duchess, or the governess, or one of the early guests.

But the open door revealed – beauty! There was the duchess, lying on the bed, quite naked, with the light of a single candle playing lovingly over her delicious curves.

"Arthur!" she sighed. "I thought you would never come!"

"Cassie!" he replied. "How could I keep away!"

"Lock the door behind you," she said, "then come and kiss me."

The major locked the door, slipped off his dressing gown, and was as naked as she was. The candlelight picked out every detail of his manly physique. Nature had gifted him with a fine body, and the life of a cavalry officer had honed it to perfection. There was not an ounce of surplus fat on him, and every detail of his musculature was clearly limned.

The captain was ready for his duel. His weapon was ready, and indeed, in its alert state was not dissimilar in dimensions to his favourite duelling pistol. He had been anticipating this moment all day, and as a result, his pistol was loaded and ready to shoot.

But at this point the analogy fails, because this duel was not going to be fought at thirty paces. This was to be a close-contact duel. Accordingly, the major closed the gap and began the fight. It began with a kind of wrestling. He hugged her tight, and she hugged him tight, and they rolled around the bed. She stroked and squeezed that firm musculature, and he stroked and squeezed that soft voluptuousness. But oh! she had a wound and it was gushing – he should lick it better! He turned around, put his head between her legs, and proved that his tongue was muscular too. How she crooned!

"Don't stop!" she sighed – but even the major's muscular tongue had to rest at last.

Then she said, "I will pay you back," and did something that few of his "lady" conquests knew how to do; something that his chorus girl at *The Pussycat Theatre* did best – and Cassie did it so well that he nearly discharged his weapon before he was ready. He thought of sad things to cool his ardour – the day his favourite pointer had died; the day he had lost a pony on a horse; the day his mother had called him an incorrigible rogue.

After a minute or two of this, he was ready to begin his attack. Now it was more like a sword fight, except that his fair enemy did not attempt to parry the thrust, but seemed to welcome it with open arms (that is to say, legs). She even shouted encouragement: "Push, push, push!" Indeed, she was so loud that he put his hand over her mouth, fearing that she would awake the whole household. The major wanted to slow it down and make it last; to enjoy this delicious duchess in a variety of positions, but she had stoked up his ardour to unbearable intensity, and all he could do was keep pounding. His pistol was well primed now and ready to shoot – but he must delope (that is to say, shoot in the air) or their affair might be revealed by the most obvious evidence of all (a round belly). He positioned himself to do it, pushing her legs aside so that he could roll free at the critical moment, but she hugged him tighter and crooned, "Come inside me!"

It was too wild, too sexy, too passionate to resist – and so he did.

"Ah!" she sighed, "hot love! I can feel it!"

A pistol has one shot, but it seemed that his pistol was firing shot after shot, each one feebler than the last, until he lay slumped and exhausted on her body. When he came to himself, his first thought was the folly of what he had done.

"What were you thinking of?" he cried.

"A married woman has nothing to fear."

"I thought you said that you never allowed your husband to come near you, and that you sleep in separate beds."

"Separate rooms – but he insists that I do my conjugal duty from time to time, because he wants a son a heir – though I can't bear him to touch me! Why don't we run away together?"

The major sighed. Why did women always want to possess him? Single women were the worse. They seemed to equate slipping a cock into a cunny with slipping a wedding ring onto a finger, then when he tried to get out of it, there were tears, or worse, hysterics. Married women were safer – all they wanted was a bit of fun – though there was always the problem that their husbands might find out. However, it seemed that Cassandra was going to be just as much of a bore as any single girl. He had only just got into it, and he was already pondering how he could get out of it.

He was about to turn over for a well-earned snooze, but she took hold of his shoulder and pulled him back.

"Don't go to sleep!" she cried. "We might not get another chance like this for ages!"

She put her hands under her breasts and pushed them up for his delectation. For the major, it was like when somebody offered a tempting fruit after a heavy meal – he desired it, but he had no appetite. She pushed her breasts up, lowered her chin and licked her nipples. The major felt a slight stirring of desire.

"Lick them with me," she urged.

He did. Their tongues met, and before he knew it they were in full *baiser Florentin* (as the French call it) or French kissing (as the English call it – there is no uniquely English expression for this delicious act because the English are proverbially reticent in the arts of love).

At the same time she reached for his weapon (which was a weapon no longer, as it had shrivelled to the size of those depicted on the cupids in the fresco above them) and began to massage it back to life. In no time at all it was a long, hard duelling pistol again, and the captain was ready to sheathe it in a well-lubricated holster.

"Slowly, this time," she breathed in his ear. "Make it last – all night if you can."

"If only I were 25 again," he said, "you'd be pleading with me to stop!"

He was 45, but what he had lost in vigour (if anything) he made up for in experience, and he took her in a variety positions that might have formed the basis for an English *Ars Amatoria* if he had been of a literary turn). He was not attempting to please Cassandra, he being a selfish lover, but to please himself. He like to pose her in a provocative position, penetrate her, enjoy her with a dozen thrusts, then turn her over and enjoy a different angle. He liked to bring himself to the point of firing his pistol, then rest a little, then work himself up again, trying to stay on the crest of that wave of ecstasy, but stopping it from breaking.

There were terms for these positions that were bandied round in the officer's mess after a few bottles of claret: 69, doggy, missionary, Roman, scissors, spoons, and yawning, to name but a few, and I am sorry to say that Major Cawthorpe was already thinking how he would boast of this night the next time he was drinking with his fellow officers. He would describe everything in minute detail, (though not, of course, details of names and places) and enjoy the jealous looks on their faces.

Cassandra was selfish too, and every now and again she would manouvre the major into her favourite position, which he called 'Roman', and she called 'Horsewoman'. This involved the major lying on his back while she straddled him and went for a ride. In this position, she could manouvre her *mons veneris* so that the major's weapon was rubbing against her sweet spot in a way that made her gush again and again.

The major was breathing heavily now, and she could tell by the gleam in his eye that he was going for the kill. He laid her on her back, prepared the way with a delicious tongue-lashing, then slammed his weapon in with such force that he would have done real damage had not the sheath been designed to receive it. Now he was like a wild man. His lust had overcome his self-control, and he could only ride his wild horse to the finish. This time it was she who had to put her hand over his mouth, or he would have roared his delight like the winner of the Grand National.

Now he really was spent. He rolled off her and, selfish lover that he was, fell asleep immediately. Cassandra watched him for a while, then fell asleep herself, but not before she had made a mental note to wake up again before dawn and renew the fight.

Etty's Venus

Cassandra was jerked out of her sleep sooner than she had planned by the sound of voices in the great hall. It was a very large house, so the voices must have been loud indeed. It was still dark, with not the slightest sign of dawn showing through the curtains.

"Whatever can it be?" she murmured to herself.

The major stirred beside her, reached out a hand, and put it on her breast. Gently, she pushed it away, sat up and lit the candle beside her bed. The major, disturbed by the light, rubbed the sleep out of his eyes, and looked at her, and after his rest was ready to appreciate her all over again. Despite her 36 years, she was every bit as beautiful as Venus in William Etty's *Venus and Cupid*. Her right arm was raised to adjust her hair and she was leaning on her left – a position which accentuated the curve of her hips, the slimness of her waist, and the fullness of her bosom. The comparison with Etty's *Venus* was particularly appropriate at this point, for the breasts of all Etty's nudes are large, but without any hint of sag, and so were Cassandra's, because she had managed to avoid having children so far in order to preserve her body for bouts such as this. Her eyes were languorous with sleep and her lips were pouting with the annoyance of being awoken unexpectedly. All this provocative beauty was made even more provocative by the golden glow of the candle which cast a painterly chiaroscuro across her body, highlighting her hills (cheeks, breasts, hips) and accentuating her valleys (cleavage, bellybutton, groin).

"A lucky chance!" crooned the major, admiring the sight before him more than any representation of Venus he had ever seen. "Now I can have you again before breakfast!"

At this point, he leapt on her, pressed his lips to her pout, and ran an appreciative hand from her right breast, into the curve of her waist, over the opposite curve of her hips, and into the furry bush (which is not shown in Etty's painting).

She pushed his hand away again – this time a little more brusquely.

"Something is wrong!" she declared, "and the whole household is waking up. You had better go back to your room before we are found out!"

"Just one kiss!" he pleaded, and by the way his fingers sought her *mons veneris*, Cassandra knew that he was thinking of much more than a kiss. She sighed with pleasure, and almost gave in, but another burst of excited conversation from the hall made her think better of it, and she forced herself to roll out of bed.

The major followed her every move, devouring her with his eyes, for after all, it was his own private show – better than the show at the *Pussycat Theatre* (for the Lord Mayor of London did not allow performances in the nude). Conscious of this, and what was going on his mind, Cassandra threw a wrap around her body, and hurried to her dressing room. Just before she left the room she said, "You had better hurry up. It might be my husband."

That thought was like a kick up the behind to the major. The last thing he wanted was a jealous husband bursting into the room and challenging him to a duel, so he jumped out of bed, shuffled any-old-how into his clothes, and made a quick getaway.

The gallery was empty, and after stubbing his toe again on the Jacobean sideboard, he stumbled into his own room and threw himself onto the bed. He decided that whatever was going on downstairs, he would keep well out of it, and sleep instead, perhaps until it was time for dinner, which would save him the trouble of having to get changed. In the meantime, he would dream of his very own Etty's Venus.

CASSANDRA RANG FOR Susan, made a hurried toilet, and went downstairs. The hall clock showed five minutes to six, and outside, the blackness of night was beginning to pale to grey. She found her unexpected guests in the breakfast room where a fire was being coaxed into life by a between maid. It was her old friend, the Countess of Collingham, and her husband, the earl. The countess was sobbing quietly to herself by the fire, and the earl was sitting opposite, looking thoughtful and making free with her husband's best claret.

"Oh, Maria!" she said. "You look done in! Whatever has happened?"

"Robbed!" spluttered Maria through her tears.

"But how?"

The Countess tried to give an account of it, but it was hard to make anything out between the sobs and the snuffles. Her husband took over and gave a brief account of the hold-up, lingering on the character of the highwayman.

"Well, Your Grace, he was a strange sort of chap – a sort of gentleman-highwayman – if there is such a thing..." he considered for a moment. "And there is, of course. Everybody has heard of Claude Duval, though until today, I thought the stories about him were a romantic exaggeration."

"A gentleman-highwayman," said the duchess, becoming interested.

Collingham laughed. "He called himself the Romeo of the Road."

The duchess was even more interested. "Tell me more," she said.

Maria snuffled, then tried to tell her how he had treated her.

"He – *sob* – and then he – *snuffle* – and he said wanted to – *mumble* – and then he – *tears* – but it's all too horrible!"

"At least he left me a stake – and a tip," conceded Collingham.

"A tip?"

"Yes, for Ladies' Day – Pretty Polly."

"And do you believe him?"

The earl considered for a moment.

"Funnily enough, I do. In any case, I will give it a try. Tips are odd things, you know. The best ones come out of the blue, and you have to go along with them."

"And have you won much at the races?"

At this point, his lady was suddenly coherent. "No, he always loses!"

AN EARLY BREAKFAST was served, and their visitors shown to their rooms. The Race Week reception did not begin until eight, so there was plenty of time for the Collinghams to recover. As for the duchess, she made a hasty breakfast, then ran upstairs to her bedroom. She hovered outside the first door for a while, sorely tempted, having been cheated of her morning's sport – but common sense prevailed, and she continued to the fourth. The house was now coming to life and an army of servants was infiltrating every nook and cranny, lighting fires, cleaning, going about their usual morning routines, but with extra thoroughness to prepare the great house for the big reception.

Race Week Reception

By the time Lord Linton got back from York it was past three, and Dale Hall was in a state of suspended animation. The frenzied activities of the staff throughout the morning had come to a temporary lull. The Collinghams were sleeping to recover from their ordeal, Major Cawthorpe was sleeping to avoid the trouble of having to get changed for dinner, and Lady Cassandra, having resisted the temptation of knocking on the major's door for the second time, was enjoying a beauty sleep. It would all start up again in time for afternoon tea at four. Soon after, the house party guests were due to arrive, and soon after that, the guests for the evening would begin to arrive, but at that particular moment, silence reigned – and that was just what Lord Linton wanted after his two hour ride from York.

He went to his dressing room, and with Benson's help, took off his riding gear and donned a comfortable smoking jacket. He looked at himself in the pier-glass and smiled at the transformation from weathered traveller to duke-at-leisure. He needed a good wash and a shave, but that would have to wait until he dressed for the reception, as it was, the dark shadow of his stubble added to his "off duty" appearance. The thin smoking jacket emphasised his broad shoulders and muscular physique, which was the result of much exercise. He was not one of those "indoor" dukes that delegate everything to others. He had a capable land agent in Stubham, but he liked to ride over his lands, talk to his tenants, and take an active interest in the affairs of his dukedom. He was also something of a sportsman, took fencing lessons with a fencing master twice a week (to keep fit, of course – these days duels were fought with pistols), and enjoyed the annual hunt even more than the annual race week.

He settled down in his favourite chair in the small sitting room to read the paper while he drank a refreshing glass of claret. He knew that, in a few hours, the house would be humming with activity, and that he would be a 'duke on duty' again, so he was glad to make the most of this little oasis of peace and quiet.

It didn't last long. The small sitting room was between the two bedchambers occupied by himself and his wife, and his entrance had disturbed her light sleep. He had not even had time to light his cheroot when she appeared in her dressing gown.

"Darling!" she began.

How that word grated on the duke. She used it incessantly, and it seemed more and more insincere these days.

"You're back early! I wasn't expecting you until after tea."

"I have a little business to see to. Dalton is coming at five – and my agent."

"But darling, it's the day of the reception!"

"I am aware of that, my dear. My business will not take long."

"What is it about?"

"The almshouse. I told you about it."

"I don't remember."

The duke reflected that that was because she didn't listen. Anything that did not concern herself went into one ear and out of the other.

"You should do your duty as duke and see about the reception."

The duke frowned. He did not need his wife to give him a lecture about his duty. He knew his duty well enough, and it frequently involved doing things that she did not approve of.

"The almshouse *is* my duty."

"How can you compare the needs of a few broken-down labourers with the nobility of Yorkshire? Race Week is the big event of the year, and it's your duty to be a good host."

She was preaching at him now, as she often did, and it seemed that she quite enjoyed it. Indeed, had she any insight into her own psychology she would have realised that she was compensating for her own shortcomings.

"I will be ready for the first arrivals. We are not expecting anybody before eight, I hope?"

"Not officially," said the duchess, "but some are here already – Major Cawthorpe, the Collinghams – and you know very well that the house party guests will come well before eight."

"I am sure you will make them welcome," said the duke, "and I will be there myself at the official reception. Now, if you will excuse me..."

As so often happened, the only way to escape from his wife's nagging – for that's what it was – was to excuse himself and retire to his study. He rang for Benson to bring the claret, sat down and lit his cheroot. But the pleasant mood of relaxation had gone, replaced by one of mild irritation. If his wife did not love him any more, and it was clear that she didn't, she might at least leave him alone. He felt there was no point in trying to relax and that he might as well do something, so, with a weary sigh, he went to his escritoire and looked over the papers relating to the almshouse.

At four, Benson, brought in a tea tray and passed on a message from his wife:

"Her Grace requests that you join her in the breakfast room."

"Please convey my apologies to her, Benson. Explain that I am busy about the matter of the almshouse."

He left, and to the duke's relief, he was left in peace for a while.

At five o'clock precisely, Benson showed Stubham and Dalton into the study, and removed the tea things.

"Sit down," said the duke.

"Thank you, Your Grace," they both said, and made respectful bows before taking their seats.

"Thank you for coming at such short notice. I will not keep you long, because, as you know, tonight is the night of the Race Week reception, and I have other duties to attend to."

He picked up a paper from the pile on his desk, glanced at it, then looked hard at Dalton.

"Now then, Dalton, what's all this about?"

Dalton was one of the duke's leading tenants. He farmed over 150 acres in Lower Wharfedale. He was a thick-set man, his features weathered from years of exposure to the elements, yet he prided himself on being a "gentleman farmer" and tried to dress the part, though a true gentleman farmer would have at least twice as many acres and would have little to do with the day to day running of his farm. His coat was well made, though old fashioned, and his cravat was simply tied. The big giveaway was below the waist, for he wore breeches of heavy tweed material, and topboots that were sturdy enough for striding over ploughed fields, and which were none too clean. Another giveaway was his manner of speaking, for though he tried to talk like a gentleman by avoiding dialect words, he couldn't hide his strong Dalesman's accent.

"Well, your Grace, it's like this. Ah've upland, which is good fer sheep, an' ah've the water meadows down by t' Wharfe, which is good fer cattle. Nah, if you put your almshouse on the water meadows, where am ah goin' to graze me cattle?"

The duke sighed.

"I thought Stubham had explained all that."

"Beggin' your pardon, your Grace, that land further dahn is not so good."

"But you will have more of it."

Dalton looked uncomfortable, shuffled in his chair, but said nothing. It was one thing to argue with the duke's agent, but quite another to argue with the duke himself.

Stubham spoke for him: "He thinks he should have more."

The duke considered this for a moment.

"I know that stretch of land, and I agree that it's not such good grazing as the stretch by the water meadows. So, yes, I can agree to that."

"Thank you, your Grace," said Dalton.

"I'll leave it to you, Stubham, to work out the details," said the duke, standing up to indicate that the interview was over.

Dalton gave a grateful nod of the head, and the two of them left the duke in peace, another duty done. He decided he would take another glass of claret, then call Benson to help him dress for the reception.

IT WAS EIGHT O'CLOCK, and their guests were arriving in droves: Lord Melton of Allerton Maulever, with his wife and two daughters, Sir Robert de Plumpton, of Nesfield, Sir Carnaby Haggertson of Haggertson, Winifred Maxwell, daughter of the Earl of Nithisdale, and many more without titles, some of them just as rich (or richer): the Langdales, the Claverings, the Maxwells and the Thwaits. Then there were the lower gentry: Rev William Holdsworth, Rev Hale, Dr Gilbert, and Mr Stubham, the Land Agent, all with their wives, sons, daughters and other relatives.

These were the great and good of the Dales. On Wednesday there would be another reception of a humbler kind for the tenants of the Wharfedale Estate, which extended for over ten thousand acres in all directions from Dale Hall, often intertwined with the holdings of other landowners.

The guests were welcomed in the Great Hall by the duke and duchess, were served with Champagne or fruit punch, and encouraged to mingle. When the formal greetings were over, and only the Earl of Egremont was still to show his face, the duke felt that he could relax and talk informally to his guests. He was particularly interested to hear from the horse's mouth (as it were) the details of the highway robbery that his wife had mentioned to him.

By the time he found Lord Collingham, that gentleman had already told his story three times over (accompanied by three glasses of Champagne) and it had grown in the telling. The duke came in at the point where he was saying: "I challenged him to a duel, but he wasn't man enough to face me, and ran for his life before he had emptied my safe. See, I have my watch, I have my fobs – and I have a stake for Ladies Day, for I should add that I would not permit him to go before he had given me something in return, and what he gave me was – a tip."

Boasting is one thing, but a tip is another. His audience, who had been taking with a pinch of salt (or, rather, a dose of Champagne) his boasts about his deeds, were suddenly all ears.

"A tip?" one said.

"Yes – Pretty Polly on Lady's Day."

"Ah!" laughed one gentleman, who from the size of his lapels and the patterns on his waistcoat looked like a dedicated turf-man. "He was taking you in, sir. Pretty Polly is a broken-winded nag at 100/1."

Collingham tapped the side of his nose, "Nevertheless..." He left his sentence unfinished for effect.

"Will you back him then?" said the turf-man.

"To the tune of forty guineas – I will keep the rest for expenses."

"What about you, your Grace? Who will you be backing?" said the turf-man who, like many others, assumed that the duke was the fountain of all knowledge on account of his rank.

"My good friend, Egremont, has a promising little filly in that race, and I am minded to support him – no doubt that is why he is late this evening."

"Daisy May, is it not?" said the turf-man. "Mmm, I might wager on her myself."

The conversation carried on in this vein for a while, but Duke Linton wanted to find out more about the highwayman who was disturbing the peace of his domains. Collingham was only too pleased to oblige:

"As soon as John said, 'It's a hold up', you can be sure that I leaped out of the carriage to deal with the matter..."

But the duke wasn't interested in hearing Collingham's catalogue of boasts. He was interested in facts with a view to bringing the offender to justice.

"Where exactly did the robbery take place?"

"Near Bramham, where the woods come right down to the road. I thought there might be trouble there. I..."

"Can you describe the man?"

Whether Collingham was being sincere, or whether he was getting his own back for having his boast sidelined was unclear, but his reply was quite unexpected.

"He was a tall man – about your height – say, 5' 11" to 6'. Broad shouldered, with a muscular physique – rather like yours."

The duke ignored these remarks and continued to probe for information, looking hard at him with his penetrating blue eyes.

"What were his features like?"

"He was wearing a mask and a scarf, so it wasn't easy to make them out – but he had dark brown hair..."

"Like mine?" hazarded the duke.

"Just so, and bright, piercing eyes – a bit like yours – but I stared him out, you can be sure..."

"What about his accomplice? Was he, by any chance, like Benson?"

The joke was on Collingham now, and the others laughed. A more unhighwaymanly figure than the tall, cadaverous, self-effacing Benson could not be imagined.

"Er, he was a rogue, a ruffian of the lowest class – but I have his name. The highwayman let it slip out."

The duke looked interested.

"Riff Raff."

The others laughed again, and took up it as a joke.

"Come with me, Mr Raff, you are under arrest."

"How do you Christen this child?"

"Riff."

"Riff Raff, you are among the riff raff of society."

"Of course, it was just a nickname," said the Duke. "It doesn't help. What about the highwayman?"

"He called himself 'The Romeo of the Road.'"

The jokers took up the theme.

"Hello, Mr Road, robbed any carriages today?"

"But who was his Juliet?

"Was there a balcony on the coach, by any chance?"

The duke was serious, however.

"Another nickname – but it gives us a clue to his character. I will see the major about this. Perhaps I can persuade him to deploy a few of his men on the Doncaster Road."

As soon as the duke had left them, Collingham lapsed into his former, boastful vein – but he had lost his audience now, as they were discussing the two tips that had been mentioned.

A MORE INTERESTING conversation about the robbery was taking place among the ladies. The duchess was enjoying a little chat with a group of her old friends, the Countess of Melton, Melissa, the Marchioness of Haggertson, Pamela, and, of course, the Countess of Collingham – Maria. They had been rivals as girls, but Cassandra, though not the greatest beauty, had captured the greatest prize – a duke – and she made sure that her friends never forgot it. However, tonight it was Maria who was the centre of attention, for she was relating some of the more interesting moments of the robbery.

"He was a real gentleman – called himself the Romeo of the Road..."

"And was he a Romeo? Was he handsome?" said Cassandra.

"Very."

"What did he do?" said Cassandra.

"He handed me out of the carriage and called me – beautiful!"

Sighs of appreciation, and perhaps jealousy.

"Did he rob you?"

"No, he said he never disobliges a lady. He stopped his accomplice, a horrible ruffian called Riff Raff, from searching my trunk. That's why I've still got these." She fingered the jewels around her neck. "But the most amazing thing was..."

"Well?" her friends were all agog.

"He asked me to dance a Cotillion. He said he would spare half my husband's gold for the privilege."

"And did you?"

"I had no choice! I had a pistol pointed at me!"

"You never told me this earlier!" said Cassandra.

"How romantic!" said Pamela, with a sigh.

"But that's not all! I hardly dare tell you the rest."

"Go on! You can't stop now!" said Melissa.

"Was it shocking?" said Cassandra.

"Too shocking to tell."

They all four giggled and Cassandra said, "Here, take another glass of Champagne. That will loosen your tongue!"

"Promise not to tell?"

They crossed their hearts and hoped to die as they had done when they were little girls, and Maria took a deep draft of her Champagne. Then she put her arms round her friends, gathered them into a huddle and whispered something.

""He never said that!" said Cassandra, rather too loudly.

"What, in the bushes?" said Pamela.

Maria whispered something else.

"That sounds comfortable enough," said Melissa.

"Were you tempted?"

Maria whispered again.

"Well, I would be!" declared Cassandra. "It's the best of all worlds: a dashing lover, but without the disgrace – after all, how could you refuse with a pistol at your head?"

"I told you," said Maria. "He is a gentleman. He gave me a choice and respected it."

"I wish he'd give me a choice!" said Cassandra, "it would be something to liven up my boring life!"

"But you are a duke's wife!" exclaimed Melissa. "How can life be boring?"

"Robert is always going on about his duty. He was at the Assizes yesterday, and this afternoon he was closeted with his Land Agent – I never see him."

"I agree," said Melissa with a giggle. "Why, I've a good mind to take a late night trip along the Doncaster Road myself."

"I'll come with you," said Pamela.

"You? I thought you were the perfect wife," said Melissa.

"I am – but even a perfect wife must do as she is told when there is a pistol at her head."

They all dissolved in a fit of giggling, which only stopped when the major joined them.

AT NINE, DINNER WAS served. The dining hall at Dale House had been designed for great occasions. It was a vast room with four great windows down one side (now curtained) with pier-glasses between them, and on the other side ranks of family portraits ranged around an ornate fireplace. The portraits showed the dukes of Wharfedale in various garbs from the cuirass of the Royalist cavalier, to the powdered wig and knee-breeches of the late duke, Robert's father. Over the chimney breast were displayed Civil War arms and armour (among them, perhaps the very breastplate depicted in the first portrait) and various crests and escutcheons, the largest being the coat of arms of the present duke which consisted of field much quartered with gryphons, martlets, chevrons and losenges attesting to the many and various noble branches of his family.

The dining table was one of the longest in the county of Yorkshire, with 80 places. According to custom, the duke sat at one end, and the duchess at the other, effectively preventing any conversation between them (which suited the duchess very well). The advantage of this arrangement was that, to some extent, it took the sting out of the order of precedence. This was a very sensitive matter, so much so, that Lord Linton often wished that, like King Arthur, he had a round table instead of a rectangular one. However, those at the far end of the table were consoled by being near to the duchess. Another thorny problem was pairing the guests. It was the custom at these receptions that, in order to facilitate mixing, a man would not sit with his wife. However, there were many jealousies and animosities that Lord Linton and Parkin, his Major Domo, had to be aware of when they made the pairings. Matters were not helped by the fact that Lady Linton had ideas of her own which, unfortunately, took little account of social harmony.

The result of these pairings was that the hot topic of the evening could not be properly discussed by those who were most interested. The duke had been trying to find Major Cawthorpe for the past half hour, but it seemed as though he was avoiding him, and, due to his being a second son, he was low in precedence and a long way down the table. Maria had been paired with the Rev Hale, vicar of St Peter's, who asked her politely about her recent experience (everybody had heard of it by now) but was more interested in making a moral lesson out of it, by comparing the highwayman to Barabbas, who was also a robber.

"But Pilate set him free," objected Maria. "Would you set that highwayman free?"

"Perhaps the thief on the cross is a better example," said the vicar.

"But Jesus forgave him."

"Only after he repented. Yes, your highwayman would make a good example of forgiveness after repentance."

"But he has not repented. Indeed, by the gleam in his eye, I think he has every intention of doing it again."

"Ah, would that I could speak to him about the Grace of God!"

"Then I hope he stops your carriage."

But the reverend gentleman was not put out. Instead he nodded sagely, as though she had got to the heart of the matter.

"I am not rich enough to keep a carriage, so he would not be interested in me – and therein lies another lesson."

Maria wondered if Cassandra had seated her next to the good vicar as a punishment for some imagined wrong – but she had no idea what it might have been.

IT WAS ONLY WHEN THE ladies had retired that the duke found an opportunity to speak to the major. It really did seem as though he was avoiding him. If that was the case, why had he arrived so early? Could there be something between him and Cassandra – but no, it was too upsetting even to consider.

The men moved around the table forming new groups arising from their mutual interests, and he was able to draw the major aside for a moment. For some reason, the major seemed most uncomfortable about this, and frowned and hunched his shoulders in a most defensive manner.

"It's about our highwayman," began the duke.

The major relaxed at once, and stifled a sigh of relief.

"I was wondering if you could deploy a few good men from your regiment to patrol the Doncaster Road?"

The major agreed readily.

"I'll send Wilkinson and Jenkins for starters. They could do with some extra duty after that debacle in the mess."

"On second thoughts," said the duke, "I think it might be better to patrol the York Road. I can't see our man striking twice in the same place."

"I agree with you there," said the major. "But there is another pair who deserve a spot of extra duty, so I can cover both. I'll see to it next week."

"Better to strike while the trail is hot. I wonder if you could see to it tomorrow, so that my guests will not be troubled on their journeys home."

"Very well. I'll see what I can do."

Of course, the major would agree to anything, the sooner to please his host and get rid of him.

But as the duke went away, he was troubled. He forgot all about the highwayman, and wondered why the major should be so uncomfortable in his presence. The only conclusion was an uncomfortable one.

IN THE WITHDRAWING room the ladies also formed into different groups. Many gathered around the card tables, some gathered around the pianoforte, and others contented themselves with conversation. One of these groups was centred around Maria, who was enjoying her moment of fame. The five different wines served with the five different courses (of course, she had only taken the veriest sip of each) had added their effect to the Champagne, and raised her to a state of confidential inebriation.

"I wish I had agreed to it now – he was so handsome!" she sighed.

"Are you going back the same way?" said Cassandra.

"Yes, and I must try to time it so that we are passing through Bramham after midnight."

They all giggled, and then Melissa announced in all seriousness: "I'm going tonight."

There was sudden silence among them.

Cassandra, incredulous, said, "What, now?"

"Yes. It's past ten, so we should get to Bramham after midnight."

"We?"

"You're coming with me, aren't you?"

"Not I!" said Maria, who, when all was said and done, had only been boasting.

"Nor I!" said Cassandra, who had other fish to fry.

"What about you, Pamela?" said Melissa.

Pamela looked around her as though she would find her answer among the card tables, then with a deep breath, as though summoning up her courage, said, "I'm on!"

Then they all broke into girlish laughter. It was the best prank they had played since Pamela (as a tomboyish child) had put the kitten in the baby's cradle and hidden the baby in a drawer.

They were interrupted by Benson who was taking round a tray with glasses of Madeira and assorted cheeses.

"Susan is bringing round the coffee, if that is what you prefer," he said in his solemn voice.

They all reached for the Madeira, and gulped it quickly in their excitement.

"But how can we arrange it?" said Melissa.

They all racked their brains to think of an excuse.

Benson lingered to clear away the empty glasses.

"I know," said Pamela. "I'll say that I want to go back for my sequined gown. My husband will say that my blue merino (which is in my trunk) is just as good, but I will protest and pout, and he will give in. Then, as the gentleman he is, he will offer to accompany me, but I will tell him that will not be necessary because you will accompany me."

They all four giggled at the excitement of it, just as they did when they were planning their pranks in the old days. A moment later, the gentlemen rejoined them, and Pamela hurried off to put her plan into operation.

She was back in no time with the news that it was all arranged.

"He has even ordered the carriage for me, though not without trying to persuade me to wait until tomorrow."

"Wonderful!" enthused Melissa. Then her face fell. "But what if we are not held up after all?"

"Oh dear," said Pamela, "that would mean I should have to wear my sequined dress for nothing – and I hate it!"

The Doncaster Road

Though it was early September, the evening air was cold, and acted as a sobering dose to the ladies' high spirits. They had not been travelling long when Melissa (Lady Melton) said, "Why are we doing this?"

Pamela (Lady Haggertson) tried to cling on to the spirit of the thing and replied, "Because we want an adventure."

"I very much fear that we shall have three hours travelling for nothing, for it's 30 miles at least to Doncaster, and High Melton is nearly as far."

"At least I shall get my sequined gown," said Pamela, trying to make a joke of it. But the joke fell flat, and soon both of them were huddled in opposite corners, trying to get some sleep.

THEY FELL ASLEEP AT last and dreamed of highwaymen and sequined ball gowns until they were woken up by a halt in their progress. So unlikely did it seem that anything would come of their prank, that Pamela murmured, "It must be Castleford where we change horses," and settled down to go to sleep again.

But there was commotion up above. The coachman was shouting and the maids were shrieking. Even then the penny didn't drop.

"A curse on these country ostlers!" groaned Pamela. "Do I have to see to everything myself!"

She flung the door open in a bad temper and stepped – into the arms of a highwayman.

"Aha!" he cried, "that's the way ah likes 'em! Eager to gi' their all!"

Pamela pushed him away and gathered herself up both physically and mentally. No – this was not Castleford. Yes – it was a highwayman – but something was wrong. She looked hard at the man, who now held a pistol to her face, and saw a dumpling of a man with swarthy features (what she could see of them) and rough clothing: a leather jerkin and calico breeches, very worn and very dirty.

"Stand an' deliver!" he said in his rough accent.

Of course, she thought, this must be Riff Raff. The Romeo of the Road was waiting close by, on horseback, covering his accomplice.

The rough highwayman looked past her, saw her friend, and said, "You too! Get out, and gerrem off – both of yer!"

"'Gerrem off' did not convey any meaning to either of the ladies, so they just stood there, looking puzzled.

"Gi' us them retickles!" said the highwayman.

He stuffed his pistols in his belt, and rifled through them, looking disappointed at the total haul of five guineas.

"Nah gerrem off!" he said again.

Once again, the ladies looked at each other, but did nothing.

"Gerrem off, ah said!" screamed the highwayman. Then, as they still did nothing, he reached out, grabbed the Countess of Melton's travelling dress by the neck, and tore it from her shoulders.

"I think he wants us to undress," said Pamela, with a shudder.

Melissa replied with a catch in her voice.

"This is horrible! It's not at all how Maria described it."

"Perhaps the other gentleman is Romeo," suggested Pamela, "and if he is, we have nothing to fear, because he never disobliges a lady."

The other 'gentleman' laughed as he rode nearer to the coach.

"Hahaha! Romeo – is it t' Romeo o' t' Road yer mean? Hahaha – that's t' ovver lot. Me, ah'm the Ruffian o' t' Road, an' ah allus 'arms everybody! As yer'll see if yer dunna get yer kit off!"

With these words he dismounted, and came towards them pointing a pistol at each one. Now that he was closer they could see that he was even more loathsome than his accomplice. A mass of unkempt hair trailed from under his beaver hat, and what could be seen of his face was greasy and blotchy. His eyes, behind the mask, were bleary and bloodshot, and his physique was so wiry that his rough clothes seemed to hang upon him like rags on a washing line.

There was nothing else for it but to strip – accompanied by an obscene commentary from the two villains.

"Nice pair o' wobblers on that 'un. Can't wait to me mitts rahnd 'em!"

"Neh – that 'un's mine, tha can 'ave t' maids."

"Oh, ah forgot abaht 'em. Come on you two," he said, waving his pistols up to the box. "Get dahn 'ere an' let's see what tha's got!"

"Ah ain't got nowt for thee!" retorted Helen, Lady Haggertson's maid, who could give as good as she got when it came to the dialect.

"Mebbie not in gowd, but tha's got some treasures inside thy gown that ah'd like to get 'old on!"

As the four women stripped, the two highwayman, as well as commenting on their beauties, and what they planned to do with them, examined them for hidden purses, jewelry and the like.

"Gi' me them rings!" said the Ruffian, spotting Lady Haggertson's engagement ring, with its large diamond, and wedding ring, a wide band of gold.

Pamela pulled at the rings but they wouldn't come off.

"Ah don't believe yer!" he growled. "'Ere, Roddy, 'old these snappers!"

He gave his pistols to his accomplice and proceed to tug at the rings.

"Ow! You'll pull my finger off if you're not careful!" cried Lady Haggertson.

"Never mind that – ah'll cut it off if ah 'ave to. But first, ah'll tek me pleasure. Nah, Roddy, you keep 'em covered while ah shag this 'un. Then it's your turn!"

"Really, sirs! I must protest!" put in the coachman, nervously, though valiantly.

"You shurrup, you!" barked Ruffian, "or ah'll shag you an' all!"

They both guffawed at this, then Ruffian unbuckled his belt, dropped his breeches, and stood there at attention.

"Nah get dahn on that grassy bank there. It's a bed soft enough for a duchess!"

Lady Haggertson, with two pistols at pointed her, had no choice but to obey. It was just as they had discussed it at the reception, except for one highly important consideration – the highwayman who was about to 'shag' her was no handsome, romantic hero, but an ugly villain, a brute, who would breath his stinking breath all over her, and treat her so roughly that she would be left bleeding.

As he approached her he began to grunt like a rutting animal. Oh, it was horrible! Better – almost – to be shot dead, than have to endure such an indignity.

She tried to push him away, but he seized her wrists, and pinned them to the ground, while his urgent manhood found its way to the portal. Then there was an earth shattering "bang!" – and for a moment, Pamela thought that her wish had come true, and that she had indeed been shot.

But it was not one of the highwaymen who had fired the shot, it was one of Major Cawthorpe's troopers. Fortunately for Ruffian, the unexpected sight of four naked women, their voluptuous forms gleaming white in the moonlight, was enough to mar Captain Wilkinson's aim. Lieutenant Jenkins did no better. However, it was sufficient to frighten the ruffians off. One glimpse at the military uniforms was enough to make them choose flight instead of fight. Ruffian saw that his quickest way was to flee on foot into the woodland. Roddy dropped his pistols, jumped on his horse and galloped for all he was worth. Of course, he could never have outrun two cavalry officers, but those officers had other things on their mind in the shape of four naked women – though, in a trice, the women had sized various bits of clothing to cover their modesty.

The officers dismounted, their adversaries quite forgotten, and proceeded towards the ladies. They made their best courtly bows, and Wilkinson spoke for both of them.

"Ladies, we are well met. It has been our pleasure to assist you. My name is... no, perhaps we will save names for another occasion. Suffice it to say that we are gentlemen, and are at your service."

Lady Haggertson, still breathless from her close encounter, said in a husky voice, "I thank you, sirs. It is no exaggeration to say that you saved my... honour. That Ruffian – for Ruffian was his name – was about to... about to... I hardly like to say what he was about to do."

"Let me help you into the carriage, ma'am."

With these words, Captain Wilkinson took her hand and helped her up. Lieutenant Jenkins did the same for Lady Melton.

"See to the horses, Jenkins," said Captain Wilkinson. "The ladies are distressed and we should travel inside with them. The horses can be trailed."

Soon the carriage was on its way again, and the two gentlemen did everything they could to comfort the ladies. Captain Wilkinson gave Pamela a hug, and seeing that he was not rebuffed, put his hand inside her cloak, and caressed her breasts – which was easy, because she had nothing on underneath.

Pamela was in heaven – was not this what they had come for, after all? Indeed, it was better! Instead of a Romeo

highwayman to share, they had a gallant cavalry officer each
– and it was dark, and what is it that the Bard said? – "Stars,
hide your fires; Let not the light reveal my deep desires", or
something to that effect. In other words, what could not be
seen, could not be known. Indeed, perhaps it didn't even
happen. The officers had not revealed their names, and they
had not told theirs, so it was all one great big delicious secret!

With this thought in mind, she allowed her hand to roam
as well, and thought for a moment that she had found his
pistol. Well, it was something long and hard. She hoped it
wasn't cocked – she wouldn't like it to go off in her face!
Captain Wilkinson felt her hand through his thick cavalry
breeches and decided it was time to draw his pistol. It is not
easy to get undressed in a carriage, but the captain managed it
in a moment. Then he sheathed his pistol in a different holster.
Pamela cried out with delight, and he crushed his lips on hers
to silence her.

Melissa could not see anything in the dark, but the moans
and groans, and the rhythmic shuffling of two bodies among
the discarded clothes, warned her that her friend was getting
something that she was not. She was a good girl by nature –
which is why she had thought of this roundabout way of being
bad in the first place. To make matters worse, the lieutenant
was a young man, as inexperienced in the arts of love as he was
in the arts of war. That was exciting for Melissa because she
liked the thought of his young, hard body, and the thought
that he had not been soiled by many (if any) mistresses. So,
shy though she was, she realised that it was up to her, as an
experienced married woman, to show him the way. One quick
move was enough to divest herself of the cloak with which

she had hurriedly covered her nakedness – not that he could see anything of it in that dark carriage – so she pulled his face onto her breasts and let nature do its work. He sucked as hungrily as a child, then she pushed his head down to her bellybutton. Then – dare she! – yes, why not? – it was dark in there, they were unknown to each other, so anything she did might never have happened. She pushed his head lower, and – bliss. His inexperienced tongue missed the spot – he just went where it was hot and wet – but that was enough – and soon she felt she was climbing into a seventh heaven of ecstasy, the rocking of the coach making the sensation even sweeter. Then he was fumbling with belt and braces, and then – is there an eighth heaven? If so, Melissa was in it! Now both couples were rocking so hard, that even if the coach had been stationary, it would have swung on its C-springs. Bodies writhed, legs twined, arms hugged, tongues probed and pistols were pushed into holsters, and all in the pitch dark in a rocking carriage – and who can say if, in their ecstasy, the couples did not get mixed up. Once Melissa pressed her mouth to lips that were so soft, she wondered if they were Pamela's. Once, Captain Wilkinson found a holster that was so tight that he wondered if he had gone in by the backdoor by mistake – a hairy backdoor, to boot! Hopefully, not the lieutenant's. In any case, as his motto was "why go in the back door when the front door is wide and welcoming?' He rolled over, found a welcoming front door and went in. It was a veritable orgy – but an orgy in the dark between people who didn't know each other and might never meet again – an innocent orgy, if that is not an oxymoron – and no-one the wiser!

WHEN THE STORM OF PASSION subsided, and they were lying in each other's arms, resting, Pamela was troubled slightly by the memory of that picture that used to hang over her bed as a child, with the caption: "Thou, God, seeest me". The captain's thoughts were more philosophical. What was the difference between this orgy in the dark and a session with his right hand? He couldn't see anything, after all, so it might as well be in his imagination.

They were all four of them brought back to reality by a knocking on the roof of the coach, and the voice of the coachman calling, "Castleford ahead, ma'am. Do you want me to turn round, or go on and change the horses?"

Ecstasy cannot go on forever. It is a thing of the moment, and between the four of them, there had been at least a dozen ecstasies, and they were tired out. It was time to call it a night, though the captain resolved that he would volunteer for many other such night duties, and Pamela wondered what other excuses she could think of for midnight journeys.

"Carry on!" she cried.

As they entered the town, they struggled into their clothes and did their best to make themselves look decent. When they reached *The Star*, the two officers made their gallant farewells, mounted their horses, and began their journey back to barracks, while the ladies composed themselves for the rest of their journey.

They made a pact to say absolutely nothing of it to anybody, and to answer any probing questions with a description of their first reflections: that it was three hours travelling in the cold and dark for nothing but a sequined gown.

Pretty Polly

The Countess of Melton and her friend, Lady Haggertson, arrived back at Dale Hall in time for luncheon on the following day. By that time, a sanitized version of their adventures was old news, and it was they who had some catching up to do.

"Captain Wilkinson and Lieutenant Jenkins pursued some highwaymen who had stopped a carriage, and they tracked down a man called Ruffian at *The Red Lion* in Bramham. It seems that the man had lost his breeches, so of course, everybody noticed him. He was arrested, questioned, and peached on his accomplice. They are at this moment under guard and on their way to York Castle."

"And I'm afraid that I will have to go there and take their statements," put in Lord Linton.

"But my dear, that is unthinkable!" interrupted Lady Linton. "Today is Ladies' Day and you are wanted to host our party at the races."

"I shall be sorry to miss the races," said the duke, "because I have made a few stakes..."

"You never told me, my dear."

"Because they are my usual. You know that I always support my friends, so I have put a *pony* – excuse the racing slang – I mean £25, on Egremont's horse, Daisy May – and I always have a flutter on an outsider."

"Which is?"

The duke knew that if he said 'Pretty Polly', his wife would say something unpleasant, and show him up to the company, so he just tapped the side of his nose, and said, "My little secret."

Lady Linton let it pass and returned to her main complaint.

"But you should come to the races with me, your wife. It is your duty."

The duke was sick and tired of being told by his selfish wife what his duty was – indeed, anything that served her needs she interpreted as his 'duty'. However, he did not want to risk a public argument, so he said nothing. Luckily, the major came in just then and distracted her, for she was full of the latest highwayman incident and wanted to talk about it.

"Oh, major, your men did so well! It's not two days since poor Lady Collingham was robbed and you have brought the felons to justice! And if the captain's description is accurate, there was nothing at all romantic about them!"

Lady Collingham overheard this remark and said, "They don't sound like the same highwayman to me. I assure you that everything I told you was true, and that the Romeo of the Road was indeed a kind of romantic hero."

The major laughed and said, "Darkness and moonlight can play strange tricks! But the main thing is, we have them, and travellers on the Great North Road need have no fear – for the time being, at any rate!"

Lady Collingham frowned. The major's answer had been generous enough, but she still felt that her friends suspected her of gross exaggeration.

After luncheon, the duke set off for York, and everybody else set off for the races – all except the major, who explained that he must visit the barracks to congratulate his officers on their arrests. However, that was just an excuse. The real reason was that he planned to run a race of his own with a little filly who was on short odds – 2/1 or better.

It was not an easy decision, because it wasn't the only bet he had on that day. The other bets were in the 4.30 at Wetherby Race Course. He had been given a good tip in the mess by Captain Wilkinson, and further enquiries of those 'in the know' confirmed it. After all, what could go wrong? Bobby Dazzler was the favourite. So he had scraped together all he could get, borrowed a bit here, and a bit more there, went to the Jews, leached his elder brother, and staked a round *monkey* on the horse (bookies' slang for £500), and it didn't end there. He had a bit left over, so he staked a *pony* on Egremont's horse, Daisy May.

Now, that would mend his fortunes – and then some! And if the favorite didn't come in, Daisy May would cover his losses and enable him to pay off some of his smaller debts.

THERE WAS MUCH EXCITEMENT among the duke's guests as they took their places in their carriages, for it was Ladies' Day, the day when the ladies would parade themselves in their best dresses, and in particular, their most extravagant hats. The duchess had had an astonishing confection sent up from London. It was a fashionable coal-scuttle bonnet with what appeared to be a rose garden on top of it. None of the other hats came close, though a cynic would have questioned the value of a hat that quite obscured the wearer's peripheral vision. Race-goers might enjoy looking at her, but she would see very little of the race, except a quick flash as the horses passed immediately in front of her.

The men were excited too, but for different reasons. The 4.30 on Ladies day was one of the big events of the week and attracted high stakes. Lord Collingham had indeed put all of his forty guineas on Pretty Polly, and several other guests, impressed by his story, had followed suit. Lord Egremont's horse had a number of backers, and there were many who swore by the second favourite, Brown Bess.

The race course at Wetherby is not as grand as its near neighbour at Doncaster, and the stands were rather cramped. Nevertheless, the Dale House party had the best places, where the men could see the horses, and the ladies could see each other's hats.

It was win-lose, win-lose for modest stakes throughout the first part of the afternoon – just enough to build up a healthy excitement for the main event. As the horses were led to the starting barrier, Rev Hale said, "I am reminded of the four horseman of the Apocalypse..." but nobody was listening. A more pertinent comment was made by Lord Egremont, who had joined them a few minutes ago. He was a well-built man of good height and comportment, strong, and full of energy, as sportsmen usually are. At that moment he was bubbling with enthusiasm for his horse.

"There she is! Daisy May – and a finer thoroughbred you'll not find anywhere! Small head, long neck, high withers, deep chest, short back, lean body, and most important of all, long legs."

"Brown Bess has a better depth of hindquarters," commented Sir Robert, who prided himself as a turf-man, "and you know what that means – staying power. That's why I've put my money on her."

"There's Pretty Polly!" said Lord Collingham, but his face fell when he took a close look at her. She was the most ungainly horse he had ever seen. She had a large misshapen head, a thin chest – so thin that the ribs could be seen under her hide, and long gangly legs which seemed to be of different lengths, so that she moved with an awkward, rolling gait.

"I hope you didn't put any money on her," said Egremont.

Collingham frowned, but said nothing, thinking it better to change the subject.

"Where have you been, anyway? We were expecting to see you last night."

Egremont bowed.

"I did not realise my company was so indispensible."

"Miss Maxwell was missing her partner at dinner. She had to sit next to the dowager in the end, and... well..."

Collingham stopped suddenly. He was about to make a negative comment about the dowager's dull and moralising conversation, but realised that, in such company, it would be a serious *faux pas*.

"I am sorry to hear that," said Egremont, "for the Earl of Egremont never disobliges a lady. Indeed, I will find her, and make it up to her; and if there are any little attentions that will make her afternoon more comfortable, I will perform them."

MEANWHILE, THE MAJOR'S 2/1 bet was going well. The filly in question was Susan, the duchess's personal maid. He had guessed from the saucy look in her eyes that she might be available. In his experience, there were two types of maids. The *ingénue* and the 'pro'. The *ingénue* could be seduced by sweet words and promises; the 'pro' was a 'professional' (or 'prostitute' – but the major hated that word – it sounded so cold). In other words, she knew that there were no circumstances on earth in which a gentleman would marry a maid (despite what happens in three-volume novels, such as Richardson's *Pamela*) and therefore demanded a good fee for services rendered. "A guinea a go" was the common phrase – and cheap at the price! A succulent serving maid, to serve his every need, and no worries about the consequences. He would not have to let her down, or break her heart – just put a guinea in her purse, and she would go away happy.

He was under starter's orders, and after grooming his filly by stroking her mane of blonde curls, and her bush, also of blonde curls, he eased himself into the saddle – and they were off! He began with an easy canter, then quickened the pace to a gallop – how his mount neighed! Then, turning her over, he lowered himself over her withers for a better balance as he increased his speed. Her rump pounded against his thighs as she got into her stride. Then he rolled her over gave her a turn in the saddle, and it seemed she had sighted the winning post for she bounced up and down as lively as jockey at the

Grand National. She took her jockey's whip and gave him the pussy-whipping of his life. He also had a whip and whipped her back for all he was worth. But she beat him to the winning post by a head and collapsed on top of him. He had not finished yet, but with a few more strokes of the whip, he reached the winning post too. It had been an exciting race, but the moment it was over, his thoughts turned to that other race at Wetherby Racecourse.

THIS WAS WHAT HE MISSED:

Pretty Polly started from the 19th post, just one slot from the outside. To everybody's amazement, she made a respectable start, but was mired in the pack for the first three-quarters of the race. Brown Bess took the lead, and Daisy May was only a length behind. As for the favourite, Bobby Dazzler, it was evident from the first that he was a false favourite, planted by the bookies to dupe the punters. It looked as though it was going to be a two-horse race.

As they rounded the final turn, however, Pretty Polly seemed to find her rhythm, and her long, gangly legs, and her awkward, rolling gait, seemed to work together to propel that light, almost skeletal body at a preternatural speed. The jockey worked with her, and chose the best course through the pack. He positioned her close to the rail, and got the inside line. As they came out of the bend, Pretty Polly was neck and neck with Daisy May, and Brown Bess was losing ground. Approaching the finish line, Pretty Polly and Daisy May were neck and neck. There was a roaring in the stands, for there were many in the crowd who had wagered on Daisy May. Egremont was beside himself; red-faced, jumping up and down, and shouting encouragement for all he was worth. Collingham was equally excited. Only the duchess did not know what was going on. Her coal-scuttle bonnet could be seen scanning the course like a sailor's telescope, but she failed to focus on the drama that was unfolding.

It was neck and neck, except that Pretty Polly's big head stuck our further and gave her a clear win. Collingham was beside himself. 100/1! that meant he would collect 400 guineas – by far the best win he had ever had. He swore there and then that he would track down the Romeo of the Road and get more tips, even if he had to hand over half his winnings (and perhaps his wife's honour) as part of the bargain.

Egremont was devastated.

"That animal should be disqualified! It's not a horse! Look at it! It shouldn't be on a race track, it should be in a zoo!"

Many who had lost their stake agreed with him, but it wasn't a valid objection, because Pretty Polly *was* a horse, even if a very ugly one.

LADY LINTON ARRIVED home in a bad mood. Her horse had lost and her bonnet had been a failure. True – it had attracted the most attention, and had almost certainly cost the most, but it had prevented her from seeing the races properly, and worse, when she had sat down to afternoon tea, the roses attracted the attention of the local bee population – and once a bee got inside the coal scuttle part of the bonnet, there was no getting it out! Lady Collingham had been rude enough to laugh at her when this had happened. It was all her husband's fault! If he had been there he could have shooed the bees away – surely that was more important than pontificating about some pesky highwaymen in York Castle!

It was she who told the bad news to the Major.

"I should never have let that mad hatter sell me that bonnet! It was too much!"

"But what about Bobby Dazzler?"

"Who?"

"The favourite."

"Came in last."

"Last!" groaned the major, feeling that his high hopes had been swept away with a word. "I suppose Daisy May won, then," he added hopefully.

"Nearly."

"You mean, she didn't? Who did?"

"Pretty Polly."

The Major's heart sank. He had not even covered his losses. Come to think of it, he had heard the name 'Pretty Polly' whispered around the mess at about the time that Wilkinson drew him aside to give him the tip about Bobby Dazzler – that was it! Wilkinson! He was getting his own back for the extra duty he had given him. The major groaned aloud. How was he going to get out of this one? He had debts enough as it was – now he had added £600 to their tally.

The Carrier's Cart

Two men were drinking in the taproom of the Swan and Talbot, one was handsome and well-built, the other tall and wiry. They were celebrating the news that the Ruffian of the Road had been taken at last.

"Here's to the 18th Hussars!" said the handsome one, whose name was Robin.

They both drank deeply of their pots, then the other, the wiry one, who was called Ben, said, "Will it be t' gallows, do yer think?"

"There's no evidence that Ruffian murdered anybody, though he was brutal enough. Transportation is my guess."

"Well, rather 'im than me. Ah've 'eard they're a wild lot Down Under."

Robin consulted his gold repeater and said, "Come, we have work to do."

They went out into the Inn Yard, mounted their horses, and rode south along the Doncaster Road. When they came to the wooded area around Bramham, Robin wound a scarf around the lower part of his head, put on his mask and was transformed into – The Romeo of the Road. In the same way, his companion was transformed into – Riff Raff.

THEY HAD NOT LONG TO wait for their victim.

"'Ere they come!" whispered Riff Raff, who was clearly the informant of the pair, and a moment later a coach and four could been seen in the distance. They hid in the undergrowth until the last moment, then rode out in front of the coach with their pistols drawn.

"Stand and deliver!" cried the Romeo of the Road in a commanding voice.

This was the most dangerous part of a hold up. At any moment, a pistol might poke out of the carriage window, or from under the driver's cloak, or a guard's holster. But it was clear at once that the coach had been taken completely by surprise. The arrest of the previous day had lulled its occupants into a sense of false security.

"Everybody out!" ordered Riff Raff.

One by one the sleepy and bewildered passengers stepped out into the road. It was a family of three: father, a plump, well-fed aristocrat; mother, even more well-fed; and daughter – as delicious a morsel as Romeo had feasted his eyes on for many a day!

Riff Raff dismounted, went up to the passengers and said, "Put yer money and yer valuables in this sack. Quickly nah, an' no tricks, or somebody might get 'urt."

While Romeo covered him, Riff Raff saw to the business of rooting out all the valuables. The footman was ordered to unpack the luggage, and my lady's jewels were found.

"Leave them! The Romeo of the Road – for that is what they call me – never disobliges a lady. Indeed," he added, with a touch of gallantry, "when they are as beautiful as you are, he goes out of his way to oblige them."

The well-fed lady looked pleased. She had heard of the Romeo of the Road, and was determined to make the most of her adventure.

"Perhaps, ma'am you would care to dance a Cotillion. If so, I will spare you half your horde."

The well-fed lady stepped forward eagerly.

"I was addressing your daughter, ma'am. I'm sure that Riff Raff here will be only too pleased to oblige. But I very much regret that we cannot make a four because one of us must provide cover."

Romeo was just about to dismount when Riff Raff shouted a warning.

"Carriage coming! Watch out!"

Romeo wheeled around, and saw, not a carriage, but a carrier's cart.

"I'll hold them off," he said.

Then addressing the ladies, he said, "I'm afraid we will have to dispense with our moonlight ball – perhaps on another occasion," having said which, he wheeled round to face the new threat.

To his surprise, the cart was driven by a slip of a girl, heavily muffled against the night and the cold. By her side was a boy of about nine or ten.

"Halt!" he ordered, pointing a pistol at her face.

"It's Dick Turpin!" cried the boy.

"Hush, Tom!" said the girl. "Ah'll deal wi' this." Then turning to the highwayman, she said, "Ah'm not afraid o' you!"

Romeo was intrigued. He had seen grown men tremble under his steely gaze, and women faint, yet here was a humble

Dales' lass standing up to him – and with a defiant glare in her eyes, to boot!

"Then you should be."

"Why? Ah've got nothin' you want – unless you want a shillin' and a dozen churns o' milk."

"A shilling and a dozen churns of milk mean as much to me as a chest of gold, for the money is not for myself. I have a higher cause."

"And what may that be, sir, if yer don't mind me askin'?" she said with a defiant flash of her eyes.

He considered the question. He knew the answer, or thought he did, but he had never put it into words before. After a moment, he made an attempt: "To rob from the rich and give to the poor."

"Like Robin 'Ood?"

"Exactly. I call myself the Robin of the Road, though a few misguided ladies have dubbed me 'The Romeo of the Road' and I'm sorry to say that the nickname has stuck."

"How?"

"Because it seems I put back into their lives something that is missing?"

"What's that?"

"Romance."

The girl gave a sneering laugh. "Romance – at t' point o' a pistol!"

"The Romeo of the Road never disobliges a lady. I always treat them with the utmost gallantry, and that is how I got that name."

"Yer not treatin' me wi' gallantry!"

"I am, because if I wasn't, I'd take everything you have – but beauty has her dues."

She gave him an arch look, though all he could see of it under the folds of her voluminous hood was another flash of her eyes.

"'Ow do yer know ah'm beautiful? It's dark, an' ah'm all covered up."

"Is 'ee goin' ter shoot us, Dolly?" said Tom.

The name rang a bell with Robin. Everybody in Wharfedale knew Dalesman Dalton's daughter, but the last time he had seen her she had been a child in short clothes. Now she – if she it was – was driving her father's cart – and in the middle of the night, too!

"Because you have big, beautiful eyes, and, no doubt, you have big, beautiful... well, we shall see. Take off that cloak!"

It was pure wordplay. For all Romeo knew, inside that cloak was a flat-chested child in small clothes – but the flashing eyes suggested otherwise.

"No!"

"Come now. Do as I say!"

"It's cold."

Romeo rode closer to the cart.

"Tek it off, Dolly, or 'ee'll shoot us!" pleaded Tom.

But he didn't shoot them. He thrust his pistol in his belt, reached out, and pulled the hood from her head, and the cloak from her shoulders. He gave an involuntary gasp at what he saw: a magnificent mane of chestnut hair, framing a well-shaped face, with large, dark green eyes. She was every bit the Daleswoman; a true descendant of the people of Elmet, that half-forgotten Celtic kingdom that had been swept away when the Saxons came. Her gown was a work-a-day garment of plain calico with the waist where it ought to be (not under the breasts, as in the latest town fashion) which accentuated her well-developed bosom – he had been right about that! Strange how you can tell everything about a woman from her eyes. It is all there, like an open book – for those who can read it.

"Would you do me the honour of dancing a Cotillion?" he said, with renewed gallantry.

The rosy flush that rushed to her rounded cheek arose from indignation, not fear or embarrassment, and her full lips were pursed with the effort of holding back some angry comment.

He asked her again. This time, she replied, "That's for the great folk. Ah only know the old country dances."

"Such as?"

"Strip the Willow an' Cuckolds All-a-Row."

"Cuckolds will do nicely, though I suppose that a young girl like you has never had a sweetheart."

"Then you suppose wrong, sir."

"In that case, would you do me the honour of dancing Strip the Willow?"

"No."

Romeo was nonplussed. No lady had ever refused his offer to dance – but then, a substantial inducement was on offer – to keep half their wealth. How would it sound in this case: "You can keep sixpence and six churns." Still, sixpence to a country lass was as good a golden guinea to a lady. It was worth a try – but with a little modification to avoid making himself ridiculous.

"I know an innkeeper who would give good coin for a dozen churns."

He used the phrase "good coin" because it sounded serious – and because he had no idea what a churn of milk would fetch. As it happened he had hit on Dolly's one weak spot, for the churns were not hers to bargain with, but her father's.

"Very well," she said, and climbed down from the cart."

"Don't leave us, Dolly," pleaded Tom.

"Ah'm only goin' fer a dance, like at Christmas. There's no need to worry."

"Thank you," said Romeo. "Let it be Cuckolds."

Cuckolds-all-a-Row is not the best dance for two people to dance by themselves. The proper dance requires the dancers to stand in two rows (the 'husbands' and their 'wives'), then each pair dances a little figure and the 'wife' moves on to the next partner in the line (thus making her 'husband' a 'cuckold'). To make matters worse, Riff Raff was covering the coach party a little further up the road, and couldn't oblige with his tabor. Nevertheless, they managed by dancing the figure, and instead of moving to the next partner, danced the figure again. It was enough for Romeo to see Dolly in motion. She skipped and tripped with all the innocence of a young lamb, and all the fluid sensuality of a young woman. Her gown was thick, she wore clodhopper boots, but she had more elegance about her than many a London debutante in a muslin high-waister and kid slippers.

The dance fell apart when it came to their turn to whirl between the line of couples from one end to another. There was no line of couples – though there was a line of bushes which might have done just as well. However, a call from Riff Raff made Romeo realise that there was no time to spare, so he ended the dance and said, "Thank you, and now – you can keep your shilling for a kiss!"

She reached inside the bosom of her gown, drew out her shilling and threw it at him.

"Here is the shilling! You can keep your kiss!" and with that, she gave him a look fit to kill, and spat in his face.

Thoroughly provoked, he grabbed hold of her, pulled her to him and pressed his lips to hers. He felt her hand fumbling at his waistband – this was it! She was going to surrender her all! But a moment later, she pulled away, took a step back, and pointed his own pistol at him.

"Ah've a good mind ter pull t' trigger!" she said. "Yer a highwayman. You deserve it!"

"Do so, then," he said unconcernedly.

"Aren't yer afraid?"

"No, because it is not cocked. You don't think I would dance with a cocked pistol in my belt, do you? I have certain – valuables – down below that I would be loathe to shoot off!"

"How do I..."

"Like this." Romeo reached forward and pulled back the hammer. At the same time, he eased the pistol out of her hand."

"Hurry, master!" called Riff Raff again.

Romeo realised that they had lingered too long, and that if they didn't make their getaway soon, they might never make it.

"You are free to go, but I won't forget that you owe me a kiss."

"An' ah won't forget that ah owe yer a ball!" she said defiantly, after which she turned to go.

"One more thing," said Romeo. "Your shilling is lost in the grass. Here is something to make up for it," and he tossed her a guinea.

She wanted to throw it back at him, but that shilling was for their breakfast in Wetherby, and she couldn't afford to lose it. So she put the guinea into the bosom of her gown, and flounced back to the cart.

"Ah thought yer wa' goin' ter shoot 'im!" said Tom.

"It were only a game. Now ferget abaht it. Are yer 'ungry?"

"Ah could eat a 'oss!"

"Well then, when we get ter Wetherby, ah'll give yer t' best brekky yer've ever 'ad!"

Then she took the reins, called "Gee up, Dobbin!" and they were on their way.

A few hundred yards further on, she passed a coach with no horses, and several people, some of them finely dressed, milling around in confusion. A portly gentleman stopped her and said, "We've been robbed. Will you give us a lift into Wetherby."

"Aye," she said, "if yer can squeeze in arahnd t' milk churns. But mark yer, Dobbin 'ere, is no racehorse, an' we shan't be there in a 'urry."

So the lord and his ladies, who had set out in such state, made their way back to Wetherby, much chastened, in a carrier's cart.

Frederick Figgit

Dolly got back to Castley Farm by mid morning – not much later than expected, Dobbin being no racehorse. She had told Tom to say nothing of the holdup, as it would only cause trouble, but he was unable to restrain himself. As soon as arrived at the house, he jumped down from the cart and called, "Ma! Ma! We was 'eld up by a 'ighwayman!"

"Oddsbodikins! is it true?"

Dolly was determined to play it down.

"We came across a carriage that 'ad been robbed, and we gave the gentlefolk a ride into Wetherby, is all."

"The 'ighwayman pointed 'is pistol at us, Ma!"

"Don't listen to Tom, Ma, e'es makin' a tall story out o' it."

"Well, that's bad enough, Doll, yer might 'ave been robbed yersel'!"

"What, o' a dozen milk churns!"

"Did yer deliver 'em all reet?"

"Ah did, an' ah've got the payment in me purse."

"Well, ah'm sorry yer 'ad to gu, but yer feyther wa' in no fit state. 'Ee nearly drank 'imsel' ter death when 'is 'oss lost. Ah told him that, just because it wa' Lord Egremont's 'oss, it wa' no guarantee it'd win."

"Did 'ee lose much, Ma?"

"Twenty pound!"

Molly gasped. She couldn't imagine such a large some of money. No wonder her father had sought oblivion in the bottle!

"'Ee danced wi' our Molly!" said Tom, taking no interest in the story of his father's drunkeness.

"'Oo did?"

"The 'ighwayman!"

Molly affected to laugh. "Now yer know 'ee's talkin' rubbish!"

"'Ee did, Ma, 'onest. Ah saw 'im!"

"Gi' it a rest, an gu an wash thy face. We've got more important things to see to than thy fairy stories!"

Then Mrs Dalton turned to Dolly.

"It's t' Race Week Barn Dance toneet, an' we'd best start gerrin' ready," she reminded her, though she needed no reminding. This was the "more important" thing that she had referred to. Of course, it wasn't the Race Week *Ball*, which was a function for the gentlefolk held at Dale Hall on Thursday, but a similar function for the duke's tenants and their families that took place in the Old Tithe Barn in Dale. It was the second greatest event in the Wharfedale calendar, the first being the Christmas Dinner and Dance.

DOLLY WAS DOING WHAT women like doing best, in other words, trying on different clothes and studying their effect in the mirror, when her father popped his head round the door. He still bore the signs of his over-indulgence of the night before in his unshaven jowls and red nose, but above all, in his hang-dog appearance.

"Is it all reet if ah come in?" he said in a thick voice.

"Yes, Pa," said Molly.

Dalton shuffled awkwardly into the room and attempted to thank her for taking the milk churns.

"Tha could've got Dick ter do it, tha knows."

"Ma says that Dick is not ter be trusted out o' 'er sight."

Dalton shook his head to show his disappointment with their lad-of-all-work and sometime shepherd.

"Aye, there's truth in that. Ah 'eard you 'ad a bit o' trouble."

"It wa' nothin', Pa. Ah gave a lift to some gentlefolk who'd been robbed."

"Our Tom tells it different."

Molly laughed. "Aye, that's Tom!"

Dalton wrung his hands and looked around the room. It was clear that he wanted to say something – and it had nothing to do with highwaymen. He hummed and hahed ('ummed and 'ahed might be more accurate) a few times, then began, in a roundabout way, to say what was on his mind.

"Ah 'ad a word wi' Fidget – ah mean, Figget – yesterday."

Figgit had earned the nickname 'Fidget', partly because he was always fidgeting, and partly because it was a humorous play on his name.

"'Ee came to see me about you."

"Me?" said Molly, pretending surprise, though she knew very well what it was all about.

"The long an' short o' it is, 'ee wants to marry yer, an' ah gave me consent."

"But ah don't want ter marry 'im!"

"Think on, now, lass," said her father as firmly as his hangover would allow.

"'Ee's t' eldest son, an' ee'll inherit t' Sickle Works at Wetherby."

"So what?"

"It's a good offer. 'Ee's t' most eligible bachelor rahnd these parts!"

"Well, ah won't 'ave 'im, so there!"

Dalton's pasty cheeks flushed red.

"Ah've seen yer canoodlin' wi' Dick! 'Ee's 'andsome enough, ah'll grant, but can 'ee keep yer, eh? Ah dun't think tha'll be 'appy in a shepherd's bothy!"

Dolly was indignant.

"Where did yer get that idea? Ah've never even looked at 'im! It's just malicious gossip!"

"Aye, that's as mebbe," conceded Dalton, "but what abaht Fred? 'Ee can offer yer a nice villa in Wetherby, an' yer own maid, an' a gig – think on't!"

The thought of the villa, the maid and the gig, were not unpleasant, but when she put that alongside the awkward, fidgety Fred, she knew they were not enough.

"Anyway's ah'm too young ter be thinkin' o' marriage – ah'm not seventeen!"

"There's many a lass younger an' you is married – an' wi' bairns an' all!"

"Milkmaids and the like."

"An' you think yer a fine lady do yer! Ah've spoiled yer! That's what t' trouble is!"

Anyway, father, if you'll excuse me. I have to get ready," she said, as her final word on the subject, and playing the fine lady in her manner of speech.

"Humph! Well, think on't!"

And with these words, he left her to it.

NEWS OF THE LATEST highway robbery was the talk of Dale Hall.

"Who was robbed?" asked Lady Linton.

"Lord Cumberland, on the way to town with his wife and daughter," said Collingham

"Was it... him?"

"It was," said Maria, and wanted to add, "I told you so," but they were girls no longer, and it would have sounded petulant.

"Did he..?"

"He began, but unfortunately, a carriers cart came up, and he had to hold it off."

"Cart?"

"Yes, driven by Dalton's daughter, apparently."

"And did he rob her, too?"

Maria laughed.

"What would he want with milk churns!"

"You told me that he wasn't in it for the money, and that girl is developing into a beauty."

Maria scoffed at the idea.

"It's not girls he wants, but mature women – like me!"

Cassandra thought that Maria flattered herself. Her pretence of being 28 would not hold up for many more years.

They were distracted by Lord Linton's arrival, and though he wanted nothing more than to wash and change, Lady Linton insisted in drawing him into the conversation.

"Have you heard the latest?"

"Yes, Benson told me."

"Well, what are you going to do about it?"

"I shall speak to the major later – ah, there he is! – but it will have to wait. I need to wash and change."

With that, he turned on heels and went upstairs.

As soon as he was out of the way, the major joined the ladies.

"You heard what my husband said just now?"

The major gave a wry smile.

"No, but let me guess. He wants me to catch Romeo."

"Can you do it?"

"Perhaps, if I use Juliet as bait."

He was only having a bit of fun, and the duchess took up the joke.

"And who will be Juliet?"

"Well, he seems to have a *penchant* for Maria."

Maria gave a shocked gasp, but was secretly flattered.

"What would I have to do?"

"We would find a likely-looking balcony – a bit nearer than Verona, of course – and put you on it. Meanwhile, my troopers would wait in the bushes."

They both giggled, but suddenly the major turned serious.

"There's many a true word spoken in jest," he said, half to himself. "There's something in that – I'll work on it."

As he was leaving, the duchess caught his sleeve and whispered into his ear, "I wish you would work on me!"

"I wish I had a chance," he replied.

"Come this evening. It is the Race Week Barn Dance at the Old Tithe Barn. He will be there. Indeed, I must accompany him, but I could not bear to stay among those clodhoppers for more than twenty minutes or so. He will stay to the end – he always does. He says it is his duty – so we can have from ten until midnight. Come to me in my boudoir."

The major was not exactly over the moon about this idea. He had worked off some of his frustration on Sally to the extent of three guineas-worth, so he could take a sober view of Cassandra's proposition – and it was risky. Her husband might at any time, for any reason, decide to come back to Dale Hall, and then he would be caught in *flagrante delicto*, and might have to fight that duel.

She saw his hesitation and sought to reassure him.

"It will be quite safe. I'll ask Sally to keep a look out and ring the bell if he comes in unexpectedly. You can be safe in your room by the time he has taken his cloak off."

'Set a thief to catch a thief' he reflected wryly, not sure whether he should agree.

She squeezed his arm and gave him a melting look – one of those looks that had been his undoing before, and would one day, no doubt, be the end of him. He gave her hand a little squeeze to say that he would come.

She went away happy, and he wandered onto the terrace to smoke a cheroot, and mull over his idea about using Juliet as bait to catch Romeo. And when he did catch him, who would it be? He exhaled a series of blue smoke rings and tried to think about the question logically: The Romeo of the Road was evidently a gentleman, or had been in early life. He must be based in Yorkshire, for there had been no account of a romantic highwayman anywhere else. It followed, then, that he might know him. Which gentlemen did he know who had been without a, what did they call it? – an alibi – at the time of the two robberies. Egremont's image popped into his mind, only to be dismissed again. After all, Egremont was preparing his horse for Ladies' Day – though what there was to prepare in the middle of the night he could hardly imagine.

The Race Week Barn Dance

Lady Linton was able to overcome her dislike of mixing with the "common herd" (as she put it, with an inadvertent farming metaphor) by the thought that it would only be for twenty minutes, and that she had a different kind of dance to look forward to.

The Tithe Barn dated back to the twelfth century. It had a magnificent hammer-beam ceiling and a row of narrow arched windows down both sides. The cows had been sheltered elsewhere for that night, and the hay had been stacked in ricks outside. Oak wreaths and garlands of flowers decked the walls, and a dozen candelabras on stands, brought over from the hall, provided the light. In the hayloft an orchestra was playing. It was the same village orchestra that played in church, with the same old-fashioned instruments: hautboy, clarionet, serpent, bass viol and two fiddles, but their tempo was a great deal livelier. The dances were the old country dances that the Dalesfolk had danced for generations: Cuckolds All-a-Row, Strip the Willow, Heartsease and Virgin's Frolic. Everybody was dressed in his or her best, simple, home-made clothes in the main, though the wealthier among them, the larger tenant farmers, the bailiffs, and the owners of businesses such as the miller and the blacksmith, had clothes made in Wetherby or even in York. But it wasn't the old-fashioned clothes that caused the duchess to turn up her nose.

"Why do these common folk *smell*," she said, with a disdainful sniff.

The duke laughed.

"That's not the people, that's the cows! Oh, they washed the place out, but you can't get rid of the smell completely. Anyway, there's no harm in it. It's a healthy, natural smell."

Unlike his wife, the duke was already enjoying himself. Everybody, whatever their class, enjoys a dance, but the Dalesfolk seemed to enjoy themselves much more than the great folk. It wasn't hard to see the reason. The great folk led lives of pleasure, and a ball was just another pleasure, but the Dalesfolk, worked hard, and had fewer things to look forward to. Indeed, for most of them, there were only three occasions in the year when they could eat and drink their fill, and sleep in late the next day: the Christmas Dinner and Dance, the Race Week Barn Dance and the Harvest Festival, so you can be sure they made the most of it. There was farmer Thompson in the line of 'cuckolds' trying his best to keep up with the young bucks, despite his girth and his bad legs; there was Mrs Adams, the blacksmith's wife, laughing until she cried at her husband's two left feet; there was Dalton, dressed in his Sunday best, this time maintaining the style down to his unwonted shining shoes – and there was Dolly, his daughter, looking happier than a debutante at her first ball, with her friend Molly, the milkmaid at her aunt's farm in Bramham.

Dolly's gown was one of the most stylish in the barn, as befitted the daughter of the duke's wealthiest tenant. She had pouted and pestered until he had agreed to let her go to the *modiste* in York, and while York cannot be compared to London, it is not so very much behind the times. Her gown was in the latest Grecian fashion with a high waist and puff sleeves. It was cut low at the front, but she had covered her breasts with a fine muslin neckerchief, it being considered by the Dalesfolk to be immoral to reveal too much. Lady Linton, by comparison provided a dazzling demonstration of London fashions, with her gown cut almost as low as her nipples. Of course, no one thought that *she* was immoral. She was a duchess, after all, and the nobility were a law unto themselves.

The duke led his lady around the room, greeting his tenants one by one. The men bowed, the women courtesied, and the duke and duchess acknowledged them with a slight nod of the head. The only difference between them was that the duke smiled warmly, and the duchess pursed her lips, as though she was having to swallow some unpalatable medicine.

When they had done their rounds, the duchess was eager to go.

"Shall I escort you?" said the duke, ever the gentleman.

"No need," she replied. "Susan is with me, and I shall be at the hall in no time."

"Very well. I shall stay until midnight, and then…"

He left the sentence unfinished, but the duchess did not mind. It was the first part of the sentence that she wanted to hear. She would be back before ten, and that gave her two delightful hours of love-making.

THE MAJOR HAD FORGOTTEN his earlier doubts, and was looking forward to a rollicking romp. His session with

Susan had filled a need, but, truth be told, it had been only a little better than he could do for himself with his right hand. She had not been so very enthusiastic now that he looked back on it. The only time she had shown any real interest in what they were doing, was when she worked him up for another session (and another guinea). Cassandra, on the other hand, was hot for him, and that made all the difference: she would go down on him, she would gush for him, she would wriggle on him, she would shower him with kisses – in short, she would make him feel like a king (instead of a plumber).

But even before he had got her clothes off, it started: the romantic talk. He had heard it all before, and he was not keen on it because it meant trouble.

"Dearest," she began. "I have been thinking..."

He sighed. It is a bad sign when your mistress has been thinking.

"...about us."

"'*Us*' was not a word he liked to hear. He was a confirmed bachelor, after all, and could only think in terms of '*me*'."

She hesitated at this point as if trying to collect her thoughts. Then she said, "We should do it..."

"I agree," he said, pulling her gown from her shoulders and suckling her breasts.

She sighed with pleasure, but even her surging desire could not distract her from what she had planned to say.

"What I mean is, we should run away together."

The major was so surprised that he stopped in mid suckle, pulled away and looked her in the face.

"What?"

"Well, we love each other, don't we?"

"Of course we do!" he replied automatically (after all, what else could he say?)

"And I hate my husband – he's such a prig. And you *are* free."

The major tried to distract her from this worrying discourse, easing her out of her clothes, pushing her gently onto the bed, and working his tongue into those places which drove her wild. She wriggled and sighed for so long that he thought she had forgotten about it, but when he stood up to remove his shirt and breeches, she carried on in the same vein.

"So shall we?"

"What?"

"Run away together?"

The major ignored her and concentrated on consummating the act, but for once, she pushed him aside, and he knew that, if he were to get his end away before midnight, he would have to give her a satisfactory answer. But what to say? His brain raced – of course, he could lie, then take it all back the next day – but wait! Here was something better:

"My love, you know there is nothing more that I would like than to run away with you so that we could spend the rest of our lives, like this, in each other's arms..." (he had the gift of the gab, indeed, his sweet words were often better than foreplay) "but I have no money, I have gambling debts, and losing on Bobby Dazzler has made things even worse!"

It was a masterstroke! It was the best lie he had ever told, and the best thing about it was that – it was true! And there was no answer to it. How could he run away with her if he could not keep her? Job done! He thought, positioning himself for the big push.

"Oh my darling!" she cooed. "Is that all! Then it is as good as done! I have £10,000 in my own name! We can go to France – no, that's been spoiled by Boney – Malta, then. Just imagine! A charming villa overlooking the Mediterranean while we sit on the terrace in each others arms and watch the setting sun."

"Did you say £10,000?"

"Yes."

"In your name?"

"Yes."

"Oh, darling, I really do love you!"

He had been turned on before, but somehow the thought of £10,000 gave him a harder hard on than he had ever had in his life.

BACK AT THE BARN DANCE, Fred Figget had seen the opportunity that he had been working himself up for. Dolly was free, and the dance was Heartsease, in which the couple stayed together throughout the set. So he stopped fidgeting with his fobs, took a gulp of Wharfedale Ale to get his courage up, and asked her to dance.

Dolly's heart sank. She would have enjoyed nothing more than whirling round the dance floor with him, if she had not feared that he was going to "pop the question". He was looking well enough. Indeed, he had never looked better in his life. His coat looked as though it had been tailored in York. It had cutaway tails and double-notched lapels, set off by a yellow waistcoat and a gold watch fob. His hair was cut in the Bedford Crop with a parting to one side, which gave him a frank and open look. His features were regular, and had a dignity that came from his position in the sickle works. He was used to giving orders, and expected them to be obeyed. He was, in the words of her father, "t' most eligible bachelor rahnd these parts". So far, so good, but when he opened his mouth, his shortcomings were all too evident. He could instruct an apprentice how to turn a sickle handle in minute detail; he could explain how to hold a blade at the grinder; he could dictate a reply to an order from the colonies; but he had no idea how to talk to a woman.

"It's a grand dance, in't it?" he began (his accent made her cringe, it seemed so out of keeping with his gentlemanly appearance).

"Yes," she said.

"An' we've 'ad a nice day fer it, 'an't we?"

"Yes," she said.

"An' it'll be a nice day termorrer."

"Yes," she said.

After that, he was silent for a long time and they worked through the set until it seemed that the dance would end before he could think of anything else to say. Fred was also aware that the dance would end soon, and was determined not to miss his chance.

"I'd be a nicer day if..."

Dolly bit her lips. it was coming. In a strange, roundabout way, to be sure, but it was coming.

"...if yer'd agree to marry me."

Dolly had her answer prepared.

"Thank you, Fred, but no. Ah'm too young ter marry."

"I'll wait!" he said in a panic, but there the dance ended, and Dolly fled.

SOME OF THE OTHER LORDS and ladies had come to the barn dance with the duke out of curiosity, and because there was not much doing at Dale Hall that evening, apart from the usual round of conversation and cards. Indeed, several of the guests had gone out to events in Wetherby, or even in York.

The ladies, of course, would not dream of dancing with a 'country clodhopper', even if the country clodhoppers dared to ask them. It was different with the gentlemen, partly because they were more adventurous (and perhaps less snobbish) but mainly because a pretty face is a currency that transcends class.

Collingham broke the ice by dancing with Molly, the milkmaid from Aunt Dalton's farm. She was only sixteen but was so well developed that the farm lads called her "milkjugs". Indeed, as she danced her breasts were pushing against the laces of her gown and looked as though they were going to pop out. Molly, though she didn't know it, was a descendent of those Viking raiders who came to settle there 800 years ago, when that part of England was called The Danelaw. She had a beautiful corn-gold hair, cornflower-blue eyes, and pale, creamy skin. Her gown, however, was quite plain, being her usual Sunday best spruced up with ribbons.

Seeing Molly's success, Beatty, the bailiff's daughter, who fancied herself, in her York-made gown, to be the belle-of-the-barn-dance, came up to the duke and asked, in her usual saucy manner, "Come now, Your Grace. Mr Collingham has shown the way, so pick and choose, pick and choose!"

She rather hoped he would "pick and choose" her, but he didn't, he picked and chose Dolly. It was fortunate for Dolly that he did, because as soon as the Duke took her hand, Fred gave them a wide berth. He went to the side of the barn to look on and wait for another opportunity.

The dance was Cuckolds-all-a-Row, and Dolly was surprised how well the duke danced it. His friend, Collingham, was all left feet, much to the amusement of the Dalesfolk, but he carried it off with a laugh and a joke.

The duke knew Dolly, of course, but he was surprised to see her looking so – womanly. In her York gown she was equal to any of the ladies at Dale Hall, indeed, she outshone them all. How he wished she would remove that ridiculous neckerchief so that he could see what she was made of!

"Was that your sweetheart you were dancing with just now, Dorothy?" he said, more in the way of polite conversation than because he really wanted to know.

She gave a dismissive laugh and said, "No, that's just Fred Figget."

"He seems much taken with you."

Dolly saw no reason why she should not speak frankly. After all, she might not speak to the duke again for another year.

"He wants to marry me."

"But you don't want to marry him?"

"Not Fred Figgit, why, if I did, I'd be Dolly Figgit – what kind of a name is that?"

The duke smiled. It was a strange reason for rejecting a man, but then, of course, she was only joking.

"What kind of name would you like?"

"Oh, something high-sounding," she said archly.

"Such as?"

"Something with a 'de' in it."

"Like my friend, Sir Robert?"

"Oh no, not 'de Plumpton', it sounds – plump."

"Well then?"

"Something that would give me a title. I'd like to be called 'lady'."

"Like Lady Haggertson?"

"Oh no! Not that! It sounds – haggard."

The duke noticed that Dolly was studiously avoiding the Wharfedale dialect, and was doing her best to talk what her father would call 'proper'. Well, of course, she was talking to a duke, and she wanted to make a good impression. As for Dolly, she was delighted to be having what she thought of as a real conversation – light, witty, teasing – so much better than the boorish platitudes that the local lads came out with.

"So what name would you like?"

"Lady Linton," said Dolly quickly, so surprised at her own audacity that she blushed.

The duke couldn't help thinking that he would like it too, for she was everything that the real Lady Linton was not: fresh, funny, and possessed of real beauty, rather than a beauty concocted with paints and powders. He smiled at himself, for, of course, there were no imaginable circumstances under which he could link his name with a Dalesman's daughter. Dolly saw his smile and blushed deeper, for it looked as though he was laughing at her.

"I only meant..."

"No harm," the duke reassured her. "Now, what if I were to petition the king to give young Fred there a title. You could be Lady Figgit."

She shook her head.

"The 'Figgit' bit would spoil the 'lady' bit, and anyway, he'd never do for a gentleman."

"Why not?"

"He has no conversation."

"A few years at Cambridge would put that right. Ancient Greats, *Cogito ergo sum*, and that kind of thing."

Dolly hadn't a clue what he was talking about, but she knew that, whatever it was, it couldn't, in the local saying, "make a silk purse out of a sow's ear".

"Anyway," she concluded. "I don't love him."

At that point, the dance ended, and the duke led Dolly back to her place. No sooner had his back turned than Fred was upon her.

"Later," she said, trying to put him off.

"Not good enough, nah, eh?" he said, with a flash of resentment.

"Don't be silly," she said, and, if only to show that dancing with a duke had not gone to her head, she allowed him to lead her onto the dance floor.

Luckily for her, the dance was Going to Market, which involved many changes of partner, and much dashing up and down the line, so their conversation, such as it was, was very broken up.

"Like ah said, ah'll..." (change couples) "wait fer yer..." (change couples) "but we can..." (change couples) "Get engaged..." (go to market – whirl down the line). "No."

"Why not?" (change couples) "I told you..." (change couples) "I'm too young..."

"You'll grow up..." (change couples) "We can marry in two years ..." (go to market – whirl down the line). "No."

"Three years, then..." (change couples) "No." (change couples) "Very well then, ah'll ask Molly." (change couples) "That proves you don't love me ..." (go to market – whirl down the line). "Ah do, honest."

The dance ended at this point and Dolly hurried away to her seat with Fred in hot pursuit. Luckily for Dolly, another young man intercepted her and led her out for the next dance, and after that there was another and another, and as the evening wore on, she began to realise that it was she, not Beatty, who was the belle-of-the-barn-dance. Not that she cared for that – but it helped her to avoid the pestiferous Fred Figgit.

Two Nudes in an Interior

It was past one, pouring with rain, and the going on the York-Wetherby road was bad. The rain had turned the surface into a mire of mud which came up to the horses' fetlocks so that they could hardly move, let alone pull a carriage which kept sinking into deep ruts. Indeed, the weather was so bad, that, for once, Mrs Langdale had consented to bring her maid and footman inside.

"If I'd known it was going to be this bad, I'd have found us a hotel in York," grumbled Mr Langdale.

"I wish we'd never come!" said his priggish wife, "for I cannot say that I approved of the play. It was immoral!"

"But true to life!" observed Mr Langdale.

"Life in town, perhaps, but I hope Wharfedale society has higher standards."

"The play *is* called *The Country Wife*, you know."

"I thought it was funny," said his daughter, Laura, a girl of eighteen with a knowing look about her.

"Of course it was funny," said her father. "*The Country Wife* is what they call a Comedy of Manners."

"I'm sorry, but I cannot find immorality funny. Those *double entendres* in the 'china' scene were quite shocking."

Just then, the coach came to a halt.

"Stuck again, I suppose," grumbled Mr Langdale. "Come on, Charles, we'll have to push."

He opened the door and was met with – a highwayman. He knew it was a highwayman because of the pistol, though of the man himself there was little to be seen. He wore a voluminous cloak with many capes, a muffler that came up to his nose, a mask, and hat with a wide brim, pulled low.

"Egad!" exclaimed Mr Langdale.

"Your money or your life!" said the highwayman.

Mr Langdale was already in a bad temper, and having a pistol pointed in his face did little to improve it.

"Neither are worth much," he grumbled. "I have little money about me, and as for my life, I am cold, I am wet, I am tired – and I might as well be dead."

"So be it," said the highwayman, raising his pistol.

Mr Langdale regretted his facetious words, and temporised.

"But on second thoughts, I don't want to lie bleeding in the mud, so here is my purse. It is all I have, I assure you. You try spending a day in York with two spendthrift ladies, and you will see what I mean."

"Nevertheless, I will search your carriage. Please have the goodness to ask everyone to step out."

"What – in this dirt?"

"Is 'ee tryin' to be clever?" said another highwayman who had just finished dealing with the coachman (by tying him up).

His rough Yorkshire voice sounded threatening, so Mr Langdale said no more and asked his fellow travellers to get out.

Mrs Langdale and her daughter made a great fuss about being rained on.

"It will ruin my best gown!" cried Mrs Langdale.

"My bonnet is soaked through already," complained Laura.

"Do not fret, ma'am," said the first highwayman. "The Romeo of the Road – for that is what they call me – never disobliges a lady. Indeed," he added, with a touch of gallantry, "when they are as beautiful as you are, he goes out of his way to oblige them. There is a cottage hard by where you can dry your clothes and take refreshment. If you will allow me..."

He put his pistol in his belt, and took Mrs Langdale's hand in one hand and Laura's in the other, and led them across the road as courteously as if he had been leading them across a ballroom. When he got to the other side of the road, he called over his shoulder, "Tie up the gentleman, Riff Raff, and see what you can find."

A few steps further on, the two women found themselves in a tumbledown cottage. A good fire was burning in the hearth and a bottle of wine, three glasses, and a cake had been laid out on a small deal table.

"Now, take off all your clothes and hang them up to dry near the fire."

The two women looked at him in horror.

"Don't worry, the Romeo of the Road never disobliges a lady. I promise – to look!"

They gasped with horror at the thought and pulled their travelling cloaks more tightly around them.

"Come," he said, "I am wet, too, so I will lead the way."

With that the Romeo of the Road threw off his hat and cloak, took off his shirt and shuffled out of his breeches. In a moment he was naked before them (except for his mask).

The two women gasped. Was it the perfectly-honed chest with its well-defined pectorals and a sprinkling of dark brown hair? Was it the flat, hard stomach of a man of action? Or was it that thing down there, which stood up and pointed at them, rather like his pistol had done a few moments before?

Their admiration of the view was interrupted by the sound of an argument outside, along the lines of: "Gerroff, yer 'urtin' me!" and, "Do as yer told, sauce-box!"

A moment later, Riff Raff poked his head round the door, and said, "Nothin' inside, sir, so ah'm tekkin' this un as me share."

"What about the footman?"

Riff Raff laughed.

"Ee tried ter play t' 'ero, so ah ses, 'If tha dunna shut thee cake 'ole ah'll roger thee instead!' That shut 'im up. Then ah tied 'im up an' made free wi' this sauce-box."

"Gerroff!" screamed the sauce-box.

"Up them stairs wi' yer!" he said, giving her a smack on the behind to get her going, then running up after her.

Sounds of screaming and shuffling came down through the thin floorboards, followed by screams of pleasure and the rhythmic thud of the rickety old bed.

"That's Riff Raff," said Romeo, "he is, well, riff raff, and he is, well, rough. So if you prefer more gentlemanly dealings, you had better remove your clothes."

They *did* prefer more gentlemanly dealings, and they *did* remove their clothes, and, as he had promised, the Romeo of the Road *did* look.

The dim candlelight gave a chiaroscuro effect that would not have disgraced one of the great masters; every curve was emphasised by shadow, every swelling was emphasised by luminosity. Take a look at that masterpiece by William Etty: *Two Nudes in an Interior*, and you will have some idea of the effect.

"Allow me to compliment you, ma'am, he said to the mother, for you could almost be taken as two sisters. And you, miss, are also worthy of praise, because, despite your tender years, you are remarkably well developed."

The pistol between Romeo's legs looked as though it was cocked and ready to fire. The only question being: who was to be first? Mother or daughter? Romeo pondered the question for a moment. What a dilemma! But then he remembered something his philosophy teacher at Cambridge had taught him: *falsus omnibus*, or *false dilemma*. It was a false dilemma because he could take them both at the same time – but not if they objected to it, for was he not, The Romeo of the Road, and a gentleman?

"Well, ladies," he said with a bow, "I have gazed my fill, and a finer sight I have not seen since the Duchess of Kent danced a waltz with me in the buff."

He went to check their clothing.

"Nearly dry. Another half an hour should make them wearable at least. How would you like to pass the time? I have a pack of cards here. Perhaps a game of whisk would suit you?"

The two women looked at him aghast.

"You mean, you're not going to ravish us?" said Mrs Langdale. Despite her moralistic lecture in the coach, there was more than a hint of disappointment in her tone.

"Not ravish, no, but if a little lovemaking is to your taste, then, as I said, The Romeo of the Road never disobliges a lady."

The rattling of the bed upstairs added point to his offer.

"How can we refuse when we have a pistol to our heads?" said Mrs Langdale, who, as a moralist, could not agree directly to Romeo's suggestion.

Romeo understood, of course. She required the necessary fiction that they had been forced at pistol point, so he pointed it again. Now there were two pistols pointing at them and it was debatable which looked the most dangerous.

The conditions had now been satisfied by which the moralist could surrender herself with a clear conscience (and she rather fancied the more threatening of the two pistols, the one *lower down*), but she could not resist a final attempt at moralising, by presenting herself as a sacrifice.

"But please spare my daughter; virginity is the finest jewel in a girls' dowry."

Laura was annoyed that her mother was being so protective. She hadn't done much to save her from Captain Wilkinson – and this man was by far the most handsome.

"Captain Wilkinson took that last year, mother," she said, "and anyway, I have a chestful of jewels for my dowry."

She had indeed a chestful of jewels, and Romeo was minded to get hold of them, so he took her hand and pulled her towards the couch. But Mrs Langdale pulled her back, as she had thought of a moral point which would nevertheless allow her to get what she wanted.

"If it must be done, I will sacrifice myself to save my daughter's honour," she said, stepping forward.

"I told you, mother," said Laura, pulling her back, "I lost my honour to Captain Wilkinson. I should go first to preserve your honour as a wife."

Both tried to go to Romeo, and both tried to pull each other back, and it was clear that a nasty argument was about to break out between them, which was the last thing that he wanted.

"I'll tell you what we will do, ladies. We will go into the room next door where there is neither candle nor fire, and we will play tag in the dark."

So that is what they did, and Romeo enjoyed the game so much that he brought himself to a pitch of ecstasy three times, but whether it was three times in Mrs Langdale, or three times in her daughter, or one in each of them and a bonus bout for one of them, he could not be sure. He could not even be sure that he had handled that chestful of jewels he had so admired, for in that dark place chestfuls of jewels seemed everywhere.

By the time they came out, the ladies' things were dry, and the rain had stopped. They dressed, and at a hint from Mrs Langdale, they pretended that nothing untoward had happened.

"A game of whisk was a pleasant way to pass the time while our clothes dried," said Mrs Langdale.

"I hope you both got the Ace of Clubs?" said Romeo with a wink. "I certainly had my hands on the two of diamonds, and on one occasion I seem to remember having my hands full with the four of diamonds."

"But I had the best card of all," said Mrs Langdale, with a melting look.

"What was that?"

"The Ace of Hearts."

Race Week Ball

"Go through it all again and tell me every detail – every detail, mind – the smallest thing can be an important clue."

The major had really got into his role as detective. He found the case interesting, and he was determined to solve it before he ran away with the duchess, for when he had thought over *that* matter in the cold light of day, it seemed an even better proposition than it had in the heat of the moment...

"He made us get out into the rain."

"What did he look like?"

"He was all muffled up. He..."

...He would have £10,000, and he would still have his freedom. Of course, he would have to treat her well in order to get access to the money, but there was no reason why he shouldn't indulge in a little dalliance – it would not even be immoral, because he was still single! But he must concentrate on what Mrs Langdale was saying.

"...took us into a tumbledown cottage. It looked as though it had not been lived in for years, but a fire had been lit, and there was wine and cakes on the table."

He was just thinking that Laura Langdale, Mrs Langdale's daughter, who was sitting there now, with an enigmatic smile on her face, would do very nicely for his next fling, when the words "wine and cake" hit him.

"Then he was prepared. He had planned to hold somebody up at just that spot, and he planned to take them to the cottage. Tell me more about the wine and cake."

"I don't like seed cake."

"What about the wine?"

"It was a small bottle, just enough to fill the three glasses."

The major sat bolt upright.

"Three glasses, you say?"

"Yes."

He realised that the three glasses meant that the highwayman was expecting to entertain two women, and that meant that they had been targeted in some way. Did he have a spy in Dale Hall, or was he, himself, a guest there?

"What happened then?"

Laura bit her lips to suppress an even broader smile, and Mrs Langdale coughed nervously. They had agreed that, on no account, would they tell anybody what had happened when they played Tag in the back room. The official story was that they had played whisk while their travelling cloaks dried. Just to be sure they were not betrayed, the 'sauce-box' had been bribed to keep her mouth shut.

"We finished the wine and cake and played whisk while our clothes dried..."

"You played – whisk?"

"Yes."

"He did not take advantage of you, then?"

Laura tried to suppress a grin. Mrs Langdale blushed.

"Major Cawthorpe, what are you suggesting? I would rather be shot than give away my honour!"

"Of course, ma'am, forgive me," said Cawthorpe.

It was a necessary concession, and did not materially affect the evidence he was collecting – but there was one thing he felt he had to be sure about.

"But the whisk?"

"Yes. It was he who suggested it."

"Mmm, then our man is a keen card player. Go on."

"When the rain stopped we went out to the coach and untied the men. The horses were still there, so we were able to continue our journey."

"What about the highwaymen?"

"They rode off into the night."

"Thank you. You have been most helpful."

There were a number of other matters he would have liked to have asked them about, but he felt it would be unwise to press them further. It mattered not a whit whether the Romeo of the Road had ravished them or not, the important thing was that he had found out that the robbery had been planned on information that could only have come from somebody inside Dale House – Egremont, perhaps? Indeed, where was Egremont?

Just then, the duke came in. "I see that Mrs Langdale is telling you her sad story," he said.

"Indeed, and her account has given me a few leads. You don't know where Egremont is, by the by?"

"He said he was off to York to get ready for the races."

"Funny, that's not until next month."

"Well, you can ask him about it yourself. He said he'd be back for the ball this evening."

"I will."

"And in the meantime I'd like you to cover all the roads in the area if your colonel will spare the men. I've got guests coming from every point of the compass, early and late, and I don't want any more horror stories. So far we have been lucky. Nobody has been hurt, and the worse victim, Collingham, is £4,000 up on the affair."

"You can count on me, sir. I am taking a personal interest in this case, and the colonel has given me his full support. I will deploy my troopers on the roads around Wetherby. If this villain dares show his face tonight, he will find himself *en route* to the colonies. So if you will excuse me, I will ride over to the barracks."

The latter was just a ploy to get out of the duke's way. It is hard to look a man in the face when you are plotting to steal his wife.

He was intercepted in the hall by Cassandra. "Where are you going?" she said anxiously.

"To catch this damned highwayman!"

"But you will be back?"

"Of course, darling. I will linger no longer than it takes to give my men their deployments."

"Come with me," she said, guiding him into a little lobby so that nobody would overhear what she had to say next. As soon as they were alone, she threw herself into his arms, then looked up into his face with passionate intensity.

"Tonight would be a good time to do it. I could plead a headache, and nobody would look for me until late tomorrow morning. By that time we could be miles away!"

It was a tempting thought. One word could secure a delicious duchess (and £10,000) but he had interested himself in the capture of that highwayman, and he wanted to do it before he ran away. In the meantime, he could ask her to transfer funds to clear his gambling debts, and thus be able to leave his regiment with honour.

"Not tonight, dearest. There are a few things that I must see to first – and that highwayman is top of the list."

"Promise me we'll go as soon as you catch him."

"I promise, darling."

"Not a moment's delay!"

"Not a moment, I promise! I can't wait to call you my own!" (When he said the word 'you' he had much more than the duchess's person in mind).

DALE HALL HAD A BALLROOM. For most of the year it was in dust sheets and the three enormous chandeliers were lowered to the floor. Now, they had been polished till they gleamed, fitted with hundreds of candles, and raised like three suns to light the proceedings. Down the north wall were six tall windows (the whole of one wing) and between each window was a huge pier-glass which reflected the light of the candles to the pier-glasses opposite, which were placed alternately with full-length portraits of the dukes and duchesses of Dale. In the centre of the wall was a huge, ornate fireplace, though without a fire, because the hundreds of candles and hundreds of heaving bodies would warm it up in no time. Around the sides of the ballroom were dozens of small tables and very many chairs, so that the guests could sit and take refreshment during the evening. At the west end was a gallery where the musicians, a chamber orchestra from York, were already playing introductory music. All the main apartments of the ground floor had been pressed into use. The library was filled with many small tables for card-games, the dining room was ready for the grand buffet supper at midnight, and the withdrawing room was ready for those who wished to sit and talk while they rested their feet.

The ball began at nine, and the Duke of York, the principal guest for the evening, was expected at ten. All the lesser guests were expected to make their arrival between those times. Late arrivals were permitted, but they would receive no official welcome from the duke and duchess.

It was a trying hour for the duke and duchess. All their guests were important people, and many of them were ridiculously conscious of it. Some expected to be announced with titles and honours that bore no resemblance to the official entry in Debrett's, which is what the duke always used as an authoritative guide. The duchess bore it well, looking forward to the supreme honour of greeting the Duke of York, though the duke was particularly concerned about his long and complex title. He was late, of course (the privilege of royalty), but his appearance was so magnificent that an audible gasp could be heard above the music. He was wearing the scarlet uniform of a Field-Marshal, with the mantle of the Order of the Garter, and several other chains of office. Benson, in his best footman's livery, complete with knee-breeches and powdered wig, had the awesome task of announcing him, which he did in his customary sepulchral tone:

"His Most High, Most Mighty, and Illustrious Prince, Frederick Duke of York and of Albany, Earl of Ulster, Knight of the Most Noble Order of the Garter, First and Principal Knight Grand Cross of the Most Honourable Military Order of the Bath, Knight Grand Cross of the Royal Hanoverian Guelphic Order, and his consort, Princess Frederica Charlotte of Prussia and the Electress of Hanover."

The duke bowed lower than he ever bowed, and the duchess courtesied as low as her legs would allow.

"Hello, Linton," said the Duke of York, as casually as if he were addressing an old friend, for, indeed, they had met several times. "Fine ballroom, this. Better than the one at Rutland."

"I am glad that it pleases Your Royal Highness," replied the duke. "Please permit me to conduct you to Pink Salon where Champagne is being served."

A glass of Champagne relaxed the Duke of York even further.

"I was hoping to bump into your highwayman, Linton. It would have been interesting to see how he would deal with a detachment of my Household Cavalry!"

The Princess took up the theme with the duchess.

"I hear they call him The Romeo of the Road, and that he is more interested in romance than riches."

"You should speak to Lady Collingham about that. She was one of his first victims."

"Indeed, I shall."

"Nobody believed her at first, but there have been two other incidents."

"Do tell me about them."

"Well…"

As the duchess related the incidents a crowd of other guests gathered around the royal pair. Every one of them wanted to be able to say to his friend and neighbours that he had chatted with the Duke of York (or that she had hobnobbed with the Princess of Prussia).

Satisfied that the Duke of York and his consort were appropriately entertained, the duke breathed a sigh of relief, and went back to the ballroom to do his duty – which was to mix freely with the great and the not-so-great; the counts and the countesses, and the vicars and doctors and their wives and daughters; to chat or play cards with the men, and to dance with the women. He hoped his good wife would do the same, but knowing her as he did, he knew that she would spend all her time with the great and the good, and pretend that the lower gentry did not exist.

He surveyed the ballroom to determine where to begin. There was Major Cawthorpe dancing with Miss Langdale. She looked quite the woman in her London-made ball gown, though, at sixteen, she was barely old enough to be 'out'. But 'out' she was, particularly in the matter of bosom, which was surprisingly ample for one so young. She was obviously proud of her new ornaments and had taken great pains to put them on display – which was no doubt why the major had chosen her as a partner.

Her mother was dancing with Collingham, but Mr Langdale was nowhere to be seen. He was probably in the card room, taking a well-earned break from his moralising wife, who was moralising more than ever after her encounter with the Romeo of the Road.

There were Lord Melton's two daughters, clearly enjoying themselves with two off-duty officers from Carlton Barracks. The major's recent deployment meant that the ball was starved of military men, who are always the most popular on such occasions. Their smart uniforms give a touch of brash colour, and their comportment has a certain dash about it that civilian gentleman can only envy. Military men have a shocking reputation when it comes to their treatment of women, but for some unknown reason, that makes women love them all the more.

The duke was looking for a partner for the next dance, and found himself wishing that Dolly were there – foolish thought! How could a Dalesman's daughter mix in a gathering like this, with the Duke of York and Princess Frederica as its symbolic head. She would be out of her depth. She would not know the steps of the dances, she would have no topics of conversation in common (he imagined her speaking of hay ricks and cow byres to a partner who wanted to tell her about his gentleman's club), and she could not even speak correct English – no, he was wrong about that! She had shown that she could when she wanted to. As for her dress, though not to be compared with a dress by a London *modiste*, it was better than many that he saw around him. All she had to do was to remove that ridiculous neckerchief and show what she was made of.

Just then, Miss Maxwell, daughter of the Earl of Nithisdale, caught his eye. She was standing disconsolately at the side of the dance floor, hoping that somebody would ask her to dance. She was a sensible, but rather plain girl, and that was why the young beaux were neglecting her – just the kind of person that he, as host, should be giving countenance to.

She beamed with delight when he asked her, and in no time they were whirling around the ballroom to the first waltz of the evening. Despite her plain appearance, Miss Maxwell was elegantly dressed and danced well. What is more, her conversation was good. They spoke about the Duke of York and Princess Frederica and about the topic that was on everyone's tongues, The Romeo of the Road. So far so good, but she really impressed him when she asked about the almshouse, for this was not a topic that usually interested young ladies – or anybody except the poor of Wharfedale.

"When will your almshouse be finished, if I may ask, Your Grace?"

"It has to be started first. There is a problem about the land."

"Not a serious one, I hope."

"I am expecting to hear that it has been resolved any day now."

"What a wonderful thing it will be for the poor of Wharfedale!"

'I'm glad you think so, Miss Langdale. Do tell your friends about it. The more people who know about it the better. I am hoping to set up a subscription fund for the maintenance of the inmates."

"You can count on me," she said, and then she changed the subject back to lighter matters, as was appropriate to a ball.

When the dance was over, the duke took her back to her place, and promised to introduce her to the Duke of York and the Princess Frederica later. He was wondering who to ask next, when there was a commotion at the door, and Major Cawthorpe was sent for. He reluctantly abandoned his place at one of the tables where he was with Laura Langdale, whispering something into her ear, and gazing down her *décolletage*. A moment later, he sent for the duke.

"We've got him!" said the major.

The duke guessed who he was referring to, but found it hard to believe, and raised an eyebrow in surprise.

"He was caught red-handed by Lieutenant Wilkinson and Captain Jenkins on the York Road."

"Indeed," said the duke, still doubtful. "Do we know the man?"

"Yes, and I've had my eye on him for a while."

"Who is it?"

"Egremont, of course! Have you not noticed that he is never present when these robberies take place?"

"I must say, I'm very surprised. I thought he was too busy with his horses."

"A good alibi, that's all."

"Where is he now?"

"In a cell at the barracks."

"I should go there, now."

"No need. He'll keep until morning. Then the magistrate can question him."

"I am the magistrate," the duke reminded him, "and I am sure there must be some misunderstanding. That being the case, I should question him tonight, and release him if the circumstances warrant."

"But the Duke of York!"

"I'm sure he will understand. The matter is urgent. We can't have a peer of the realm under lock and key unless there is a case against him."

"I tell you, he was caught red-handed. Wilkinson says that he tried to hold up a Mr Tomlinson and his wife who were on their way to York. The footman fired at him, and the shot attracted the lieutenant and his company."

"Nevertheless, I should go. Will you join me?"

"Forgive me, Your Grace, but I think the matter will wait until the morning."

"Very well," said the duke with a resigned sigh. He knew that he should do his duty, and as the major was not directly involved, there was no reason why his evening should be spoiled too. So he went to give his apologies to the Duke of York, and thereafter to call for his horse.

In a moment, the news was everywhere, and it made such an impression that the Duke of York himself made a short speech congratulating the major.

"It shows what we military men can do when we set our minds to it. Three cheers for the major!"

There were three cheers, after which the orchestra struck up the National Anthem, followed by another waltz in which the Duke of York and the Princess Frederica took the lead, and the Duchess of Wharfedale, with the major standing in for the duke, followed behind. After a turn around the dance floor, the others were invited to join in.

"Now it is time to keep your word," whispered the duchess. "There will never be a better opportunity. Everybody will be occupied with the ball until the early hours, and my husband will not be back until after midnight at the earliest, and probably not until tomorrow morning."

The major was flushed with triumph. He had got his man, and now he was going to get his £10,000 pounds.

"I'm on!" he whispered.

"Darling!" she crooned, almost forgetting herself and giving him a kiss in public, but she remembered where she was just in time, and kept her distance while telling him her plan in a low voice.

"I will arrange for the dowager's carriage to be brought to the door at midnight. No-one will remark it. They will simply assume, if they bother to assume anything, that she is going home to the dower house. Of course, she is staying here, so we need not worry about her. I will get into it and it will pick you up halfway down the drive where the elm trees begin. We will go as far as Wetherby, then travel by post chaise to London. The coachman will return the dowager's coach to the stables and no-one will be the wiser. By the time they realise we are gone, we shall be in Stamford, or further. Sally will remain on guard outside my room, and will prevent people from disturbing me as long as possible"

"What about our things?"

"I shall make do with a portmantle, and you should do the same. There is no time for anything else. You can come as you are. We can buy anything we need as we travel."

The word 'buy' sounded good to the major, so he agreed to the plan without hesitation. All that remained was to while away the evening until twelve o'clock, and that was best done out of each other's company. He decided to smoke a cheroot on the terrace to mull over his change of fortune and plan how to spend that £10,000 pounds, and the duchess decided on a quiet game of whisk in the card room with her three old friends.

The Prisoner

"**A**m I glad to see you!" said Egremont, who was sitting disconsolately in the corner of a damp and dirty cell.

"Don't worry. I'll get you out of here, but there is a process to go through," said the duke, with comforting confidence.

"You believe me then?"

"You haven't told me anything to believe or disbelieve, but I am certain that you are not a highwayman – indeed, the idea is ridiculous!"

"Thank God for that!" said Egremont, standing up to leave.

"Wait, old friend. I'm here in my capacity as a magistrate, and I'm going to question the witnesses to see if there is a case to prosecute."

"But you said you believed me!"

"The purpose of the questioning is to establish that you are innocent. Then I can order your release."

A guard led them into an adjoining room containing nothing but a large table and several chairs. The lieutenant, the captain, Mr Tomlinson, his footman, and the coachman were all seated round the table as the duke had requested. He took his seat at the head of the table, and Egremont, still under guard, was seated at the other end.

"Gentlemen," began the duke. "Thank you for assembling here at this late hour, but Lord Egremont is a Peer of the Realm and it is incumbent on me as the local magistrate to enquire if there is sufficient evidence for a prosecution. Coachman, I think you were the first to see the accused. Will you tell us what you saw."

"We was goin' along t' York Road towards York, a few mile outside Wetherby, when ah saw a figure in t' distance. His face wa' muffled up an' 'ee looked suspicious. So ah says to Ted, 'ere, 'Watch aht!' an' before ah knew it – 'bang', off goes 'is pistol."

"It's a good job he missed or we might be here on a murder charge," commented the duke.

Edward, the footman, shuffled uneasily.

"Now tell me, Edward," the duke continued, "why you fired at Lord Egremont."

"I thought 'ee wa' a 'ighwayman," Edward replied simply.

"Was he wearing a mask?"

"No, but they don't all wear masks."

"Was he pointing a pistol?"

"Yes."

"That's not true!" interrupted Egremont. "I only drew my pistol *after* I was shot at."

"Coachman?"

"That's reet, Your Grace."

"A question for both of you, and Mr Tomlinson; did the accused at any time make a threat or a demand."

"'Ee might 'ave," said Richard, "but 'ee wa' too far away fer us to 'ear."

The duke dismissed that piece of nonsense with a "humph", then turned to the lieutenant.

"Lieutenant, what is your version of events?"

"We heard a shot, and galloped up to find out what was going on, and we found this man with his pistol drawn, pointing at Mr Tomlinson's carriage."

The duke pondered what he had heard – more for the effect of it than because he needed to think things through, because the conclusion was obvious.

"Lord Egremont has no case to answer. It is clear that he was mistaken for a highwayman, and a nervous footman – you, Edward – shot at him without due cause. He was not masked, he was not drawn, and he issued no threat or demand. Case dismissed."

No one objected to the verdict, though there was disappointment all round that the highwayman was still on the loose, and that all their hard work, and their late-night meeting, had been for nothing.

THE DUKE WAS EXHAUSTED after hosting the ball, riding to Wetherby, and cross-examining the witnesses to Egremont's supposed hold-up, but a duke has his duty, and his duty now was to his guests. So he hauled his weary body onto his horse and set out for Dale Hall.

It was past one when he arrived, and several of the guests had left, and some of his house party guests had retired to bed, including the Duke of York and the Princess Frederica, but the ball was till in full swing. Revived by the Champagne Supper, the young people were still whirling around the dance floor, and their elders were looking on or playing cards.

The first thing the duke did was to ask for the major, but nobody had seen him for a while.

"He must have gone to bed," said Collingham.

"That's not like Cawthorpe," commented Haggertson, "he's usually playing cards all night, and finds his way to bed when everybody else is getting up."

"Unless," said Collingham, "he has found a better game to play."

"Better game?"

"The game of Cupid – shoot his arrow into some young woman's... well, we are mixed company. I will say no more."

"Yes, that's probably it," said Haggertson. "Any news about the highwayman?"

"It was all a mistake," said the duke. "A nervous footman shot at an innocent horseman, and that horseman happened to be my friend Egremont."

"Pity," said Haggertson. "Glad Egremont's in the clear, though."

"Have you seen the duchess?" asked the duke.

"She went to bed before supper, pleading a headache."

"Very well. Now, if you will excuse me, I must change."

The duke went to their private sitting room, and found Susan asleep on the couch. He was just about to open the duchess's bedroom door, when Susan, disturbed by his entrance, said, "My Lady said not to disturb her, if you please, Your Grace, as she has a headache."

"Very well then. My news will wait until morning," said the duke, and went into his own dressing room instead. He rang for Benson, got changed, then, tired though he was, went downstairs to the ballroom to play host until the last of his guests crept up to bed – and that would not be until dawn had broken.

WHEN THE FIRST GLIMMER of grey peeped through the gaps in ballroom curtains, the duke deemed that he had done his duty for now and could rest for an hour before entertaining the royal couple at breakfast and helping them prepare for their departure. After an encouraging word to the few remaining people who still seemed to be able to stand up straight enough to dance, and a generous tip to the musicians (who had kept going by playing in shifts), he made his way up the Great Staircase to their private sitting room.

Susan was still there, soundly asleep on the couch, but the duke saw no need to wake her. A quick word was all he wanted, to warn his wife that she would need to be up and dressed in a hour. He tried the door, but it was locked, so he knocked gently. There was no reply, and he assumed that his wife must be sleeping deeply. Nevertheless, he felt that it was important to remind her, knowing that she would be furious if he allowed her to sleep through the Duke of York's departure. He rapped loudly and called her name, but there was still no reply. Then he noticed that Susan had woken up and was sobbing.

"It's no good, Your Grace, she's not there."

"What do you mean?"

"She's gone! Run off with the major."

"Damn and blast that man!" growled the duke.

He prided himself that he never swore in front of a woman, but under these circumstances he excused himself, and hurried to his study to fetch his master key. He unlocked the door, and found that what Susan had said was true; the room was empty. The horror of it almost overwhelmed him. Six generations of the dukes of Wharfedale had been brought into disgrace at a stroke, and he, personally, had been humiliated. It had never been a love match, rather an arranged marriage in which the principal factors were money, property, and his title – but how many of the nobility had the luxury of marrying for love? It was expected that man and wife would get on together like good friends, and would learn to love each other in a deeper and more fulfilling way that the transient passion of romantic love. Cassandra, however, had never been able to accept that. She had some impossible romantic dream which tormented her, and she blamed him for its lack of fulfilment. Well, it was over now, and she was gone. All he could think of at that moment was to preserve the honour of his house for a few more precious hours until the Duke of York had been seen safely on his way.

He questioned Susan further, but all he could discover was that they had left at midnight in the dowager's coach. The dowager's coach was a stately old thing, and he guessed that they would have travelled post from Wetherby – and it was now too late to overtake them. He made Susan promise to stay where she was and tell anyone who came that the duchess was indisposed and not to be disturbed, and then with a heavy sigh, he resumed the mantle of his duke's duty for the last time.

WHEN THE DUKE OF YORK and the Princess Frederica had made their departure, most of their house party guests made theirs, By midday only a few old friends remained, among them, Egremont, and the duke knew what he had to do. He realised that it was far better to tell everybody himself than let them find out through the rumour machine, so he gathered them into the withdrawing room and told them everything he knew about the duchess's elopement. It was a terrible moment for him: he felt upset, embarrassed and humiliated, but somehow he got through it.

"Ecod!" exclaimed Egremont, "that's the worse thing that's happened since – well, since I was arrested for highway robbery!"

The duke replied sadly, "but it will no be so easily solved. I must go to London to try to sort out this difficult matter. Indeed, there is another reason: I could not bear people's condolences, and even worse would be the false condolences followed by laughing behind my back. Therefore, I am going to shut up the house. I will need Benson with me, so Parkin will be in charge of the household. Stubham, my Land Agent, will take care of the affairs of my estate. If you need to contact me, you can write to me at my town house in Edward Street."

"If there is anything I can do to help, Linton, you can call on me," said Egremont. "I speak as a friend, and not just because you saved me from that rat-infested cell."

There were other, similar, offers of help – most just empty words, but a few of which were equally sincere.

"Gentleman, ladies, I thank you for your indulgence in hearing me out. It is my desire to leave this place as soon as possible, so if you will excuse me..."

With these words, the duke left the room and went to make the necessary arrangements.

AFTER THE DUKE HAD gone, the Wharfedale estates languished. Stubham continued to give good and loyal service, but he did not have the authority to order repairs or investments, so productivity declined and complaints went up. The plan for the new almshouse was forgotten, and the old almshouse had to be pulled down before it fell down, so the elderly and infirm among the Dalesfolk had no other recourse than to beg for their bread in the streets of Wetherby. Nor was there anyone to see to the policing of the highways. The duke and the major, though bitter rivals, had worked together to good effect, but now the highwaymen had it all their own way – and most of them were as unlike The Romeo of the Road as could be – they were out and out villains, who would maim and kill without hesitation to get what they wanted. The people of Wharfedale had barely noticed their duke when he was there, had no idea of all the things he did on their behalf, and had taken for granted his benevolent, if paternalistic, presence. But when he was gone, he was sorely missed, for they realised that their lord and master was a rare being indeed – a duke who did his duty.

Another Barn Dance

It had been raining all day and the York road was a quagmire. The drag from the Queen's Seminary was making slow progress on its return journey from York, where the girls had been taken to watch a performance of Shakespeare's *Midsummer Night's Dream*. It was only ten o'clock, and Miss Pringle's only concern was that they would not get back to the seminary until after 'lights out', which would mean disturbing everybody. She knew that the York road was notorious for highwaymen, but believed that they only attacked after midnight – and in any case, what would be the point in holding up a drag full of schoolgirls? The most they could hope to get would be a sackful of cheap trinkets and an assortment of coins of low denominations.

So she was more surprised than frightened when a passing horseman wheeled around in front of the drag and demanded: "Stand and deliver!"

Most of the girls would scream if they saw a spider, and a highwayman is infinitely more horrible than that, so it was hard for Miss Pringle to make herself heard over the noise.

"Sir, you must have got the wrong conveyance!" she shouted. "This is the Queen's Seminary drag. It is full of schoolgirls, and I doubt that they could raise as much as one guinea between them."

"The Romeo of the Road, for that is what they call me, is interested in other things than money. My accomplice here will, however, be glad of the guinea."

"How shocking, and how cowardly, to pick on a poor parcel of schoolgirls! You can be sure that I shall inform the headmistress!"

That threat did little to deter Romeo who, if anything, seemed rather amused at the idea of a strict headmistress giving him a good dressing down (and, perhaps, a good thrashing with her rattan cane).

"Take your girls into that barn across the road," he said with a laugh, then turning to Riff Raff said, "Tie up the driver, then follow us, and don't forget Punch and Judy."

The barn had been prepared for their reception. The floor had been cleared, and candles and been lit. As soon as the girls were assembled, Romeo said, "I am minded to engage you all in a barn dance – hence the barn – and to add spice to the occasion, it will be a naked barn dance!"

The girls responded with an ear-splitting scream.

"No all of you, of course," continued the highwayman. "Those who are under 16 should go to the cow byre next door where Riff Raff will entertain you with a Punch and Judy show."

He waited until the younger girls had gone, then said to the others, "Now take off your clothes."

Some began to strip with alacrity, seeing it as a bit of fun, but most of them hugged each other and wept.

"Stop!" shouted Miss Pringle.

They stopped. Miss Pringle's word was law in the seminary.

"Jessica, you are not sixteen, far from it. Now go and watch the Punch and Judy show!"

"Please Miss, I saw Punch and Judy at Scarborough last summer. I want to see the show here!"

"Do as I tell you instantly, or I will give you a hundred lines."

Jessica, with a big pout on her face, went to the Punch and Judy show.

"Thank you ma'am," said the highwayman with a bow. "I would never want it to be said that the Romeo of the Road is a cradle-snatcher."

"I hope you are not going to snatch anybody!"

Romeo winked.

"It depends what you mean by 'snatch' – all I had in mind is a barn dance, a naked barn dance, so come on girls – strip!"

"No!" said Miss Pringle. "Spare my girls! You can do what you like with me, but – spare my girls!"

Romeo looked her over. Miss Pringle's hair was gathered into a stern bun, and her features were equally stern, no doubt from frequent schooling of her features into an expression that would command obedience. Yet it was a well-formed face with large grey eyes and a determined chin. Her body was well-formed too, what could be seen of it under her voluminous travelling dress.

With bow that would not have disgraced a courtier, he said, "The Romeo of the Road never disobliges a lady. Indeed," he added, with his customary touch of gallantry, "when they are as beautiful as you are, he goes out of his way to oblige them."

The girls giggled, so turning to towards them, Romeo said, "I hope you appreciate the sacrifice that your teacher is making in your behalf."

"It's no sacrifice, she's gagging for it!" said one ungrateful urchin under her breath.

The girls giggled again.

"I know that voice, Pamela Parsons. Take a hundred lines," said Miss Pringle, "and there will be a hundred more for any other girl who does not do as she is told. Now, be quiet, and go an watch the Punch and Judy show while I – sacrifice myself."

The girls obeyed and filed out in silence to the cow byre. When they had gone, Romeo took Miss Pringle into the hayloft. However, two girls, who should have been watching Punch pummel Judy, sneaked back into the barn to watch Romeo pummel Miss Pringle – it was quite a show!

They could hear the other girls jeer when Punch produced his truncheon, but when Romeo did the same, they gasped with surprise and horror.

"It's so big!" hissed Bella, in a whisper.

"He'll never get it in!" Della hissed in reply.

"It's horrible! I'd rather go into a nunnery!"

"You got the hairbrush handle in!"

"But it wasn't as big as that!"

The small girls jeered again as Punch hit Judy over the head with his truncheon. Romeo didn't do that exactly, but he put it in her face.

"What's he doing now?" whispered Bella.

"She's going to eat it!" whispered Della.

"She's sucking it like a lollipop."

"What if he…" but she couldn't bring herself to say it.

Punch was now beating Judy on the behind. Romeo turned Miss Pringle over and threw up her gown.

"Golly! It's like two moons!" said Bella.

"That's why they call it a moonie," said Della.

"What's he doing now?"

"He's going to do it like a doggy!"

"That's disgusting! We're not animals!"

"Yes we are. Our biology teacher says that we're mammals."

"Well if we are, I'm going into that nunnery. That doesn't look nice at all!"

"But Miss Pringle seems to be enjoying it!"

And it was true, for if Judy was whimpering with pain in the Punch and Judy show, Miss Pringle was whimpering with pleasure.

There was a cheer from the cow byre because Judy had snatched the truncheon from Punch and was beating him with it, and at the same time, Miss Pringle had taken out her rattan cane and started to beat Romeo with it.

"Ugh!" said Bella with disgust. "His moons are all hairy!"

"That's because he's a mammal."

"Like a gorilla?"

"A bit."

"Why is he letting her do it? He's twice as strong as she is?"

"Keep your voice down or it'll be our turn next."

Now there was a jeer from the cow byre because Punch had got the truncheon again and was belabouring Judy soundly.

In the hayloft, Romeo was smacking Miss Pringle's creamy moons, first with his hand, and then with his truncheon. Then he turned her over and his truncheon slid into Miss Pringle's bush.

"I can see it better, now," whispered Bella.

"Me too. It's gone in all the way," whispered Della.

"Do you think he'll be able to get it out again?"

"It's coming out, now."

And that was because Romeo was turning Miss Pringle over. In the cow byre, the small girls were laughing because Judy was giving Punch a whipping, and now Miss Pringle was giving Romeo a pussywhipping such as he'd never had in his life. The small girls cheered Judy on, and Bella cheered Miss Pringle on.

"Go, go, go! Miss Pringle. I respect you now. I'll never be cheeky to you again!"

"Shhhhh!"

But it was too late. Miss Pringle had finished meting out her punishment of pleasure, and had rolled off Romeo to fall asleep at his side. But where was Romeo?

A moment later, a hand seized each girl by the scruff of their necks.

"I hope you enjoyed the show, girls," laughed Romeo, "because you're next!"

He was joking, of course, because The Romeo of the Road would never take advantage of a lady, particularly a young, inexperienced lady, however curious she was.

TWO DAYS LATER, THE Rev Hale was on his way to York Minster with a donation for the Indian Mission which had been dutifully collected over the past six months at St Peter's, and amounted to over £25.

The first he knew of the hold-up was when the coach stopped suddenly and a masked ruffian opened the door and held a pistol to his head.

"Yer money or yer life!" he said in a broad accent.

"Sir, the money I have is not mine, but God's," retorted the reverend, with just indignation. "It is intended for the purpose of converting poor misguided Mussulmen in India."

The rogue seemed to find that funny. He grabbed the vicar's purse, glanced inside it and said, "'Ow much?"

"£25 14s 9d – donated, I should say, by ordinary Dalesfolk folk in the hope of saving the souls of their less fortunate brethren."

"Good – it saves me t' trouble o' robbin' 'em one by one!"

The vicar shook his head and pronounced stern judgement on the malefactor.

"Does not the prophet Malachi say, 'Ye are cursed with a curse: for ye have robbed me, even this whole nation'?"

The highwayman obviously didn't understand a word of this, so the vicar tried something simpler.

"Exodus, Chapter 20, Verse 16: 'Thou shalt not steal'. I think that's clear enough even for you!"

The highwayman didn't find *that* funny – but he didn't give the collection back, either.

The vicar made one last effort: "Think, man! It is your immortal soul that is in peril! Here, take my pocketbook instead. There is five pounds in there. Rob me of that, if you will, and The Lord may forgive you, but rob God of his dues and I fear for your soul."

The highwayman looked troubled, but it didn't stop him from taking the vicar's pocketbook and stuffing it into his booty bag.

"And now, perhaps..." began the vicar, hoping the ordeal was over.

"Ah've not finished with yer, yet," said the highwayman. "Get them togs off!"

"I beg your pardon."

"Tek yer clothes off. Ah wants 'em!"

Poor Rev Hale had no choice but to obey. After which, he was tied up, back to back, with the coachman, in nothing but his Long Johns.

ABOUT AN HOUR LATER, not far away, a clergyman waved down a carriage carrying a lady and her maid. He asked for a lift and was invited into the carriage. About a mile further on, he got out again with six guineas in cash, and jewellery worth over £100. From that day on, the Reverend Rogue, as he came to be known, became the curse of the Great North Road.

Britney

The major's elopement with the duchess took place so precipitously that he quite forgot to clear his debts of honour, not to mention his mess bill. The result was that he was cashiered *in absentia*, and the value of his commission defaulted to the regiment. It was offered to Lieutenant Wilkinson at a discount, who was delighted to secure an early promotion on such good terms.

The major was halfway across the Atlantic when he remembered this oversight, and by that time, it was too late. He would have preferred to have cleared his debts before he had left, because that would at least have preserved his honour in the mess – private peccadillos, especially with women, being more likely to lead to praise rather than blame. He would still have been cashiered because he was, in the military term, AWOL (absent without leave). Leave was not difficult to get if you were a major (indeed, he spent most of his time on leave of one sort or another) but to just disappear without a word to anyone would not be tolerated.

So the major leaned over the rail of the Armed Frigate, *Nymphe*, trying to accept that he was a major no longer. It was not easy. Being a military man was part of his life. At 18, his father had said to him, "There's not much I can do for you, son, the family fortunes being what they are, but I can buy you a commission as a cornet, and if you do your duty, I'll see what can be done about promotion when the time comes."

He took to the life like a duck to water, his only problem being lack of funds. An officer is a gentleman, and a gentleman never thinks of money. He has a competence, of course, quite apart from his army pay, and is expected to spend it generously on claret, cards, horses and women. But poor Cawthorpe had to borrow to keep up, which meant that his enjoyment of the military life was always under a shadow – no wonder that the duchess's offer was impossible to resist.

He felt a light touch on his arm, and knew that she had joined him at the rail. She heaved a sigh and surveyed the rolling blue-grey emptiness, thinking, perhaps, of the emptiness in her heart. She had given up everything for this man – or to put it another way, she had given up everything for her dream of love, and just now, it seemed a poor bargain. In Wharfedale she had been mistress of all she surveyed: she had been admired, respected, sought-after. She had played hostess to the leading families in Yorkshire, and even to royalty. But who was she now? Just an unknown woman on a ship – but love! It was worth it for love! That was what she had yearned for all her life, and she had found it at last. She slid her arm round Arthur's waist, and he felt her need, and held her tight.

"It will be all right, won't it, Arthur?" she said with a catch in her voice.

He squeezed her tighter and said, "Of course it will, my darling. Of course it will."

THEY FOUND A VILLA overlooking the sea on the North Shore of the island next to the Governor's residence – not that you could see the residence itself, just a plantation of Bermuda Palmettos that seemed to go on forever before you came to the house itself. Nevertheless, Cassandra was delighted to think that the governor was just next door, and imagined many delightful receptions and soirées at which she would play a leading part. Arthur was pleased too, because it was not far from Warwick Camp Barracks, the headquarters of the Bermuda Garrison, and only a short ferry crossing from the Royal Naval Dockyard, which was busier than ever due to the war with America.

The villa was called *Britney*, probably named after the home country by some home-sick expatriate. Like most Bermuda houses, it was a low, square building with a stepped, white roof and pastel-painted walls, both of which were made out of stone – a design that had evolved to withstand hurricanes. At the front was a porch and a verandah, and it was here that the lovers would sit for hours, watching the ships of the line go in and out of the Royal Naval Dockyard, and enjoying the soporific effect of the heat and humidity while they sipped gin and tonic, the preferred refreshment for British expatriates in hot climates. It was served by Abigail, their maid-of-all-work, a cheerful fifteen-year-old of Carib stock. In addition to Abigail, they had Abe, whom Arthur adopted as his manservant, a boy-of-all-work whom they called Boy, and a cook called Bertha.

The 'dark night of the soul' that had visited both of them in mid-Atlantic was forgotten now, as it seemed they had arrived in a tropical paradise. The vegetation was lush, the pastel-painted buildings pretty, and the beaches – quite magically it seemed – were pink. Arthur was confident that he could find a role in the Bermuda Garrison or the Naval Staff, so that feeling of a loss of identity ceased to trouble him, and he was fortified by a comforting sense of £10,000 at his disposal. Also, there was that sense of endless possibilities which always comes with new beginnings. To take just one example: his front garden ended in a low cliff into which steps had been cut that led down to a small jetty – the perfect arrangement for keeping a yacht. Yes, he would take up sailing, and get to know some of the naval officers just across the Great Sound.

Cassandra was also in good spirits. She was looking forward to a reception at the Governor's House, where, as newly arrived British subjects, they would be guests of honour. They had adopted the name Thorpe, and while plain Mrs Thorpe was quite a comedown from Lady Linton, at least she would have the man of her dreams by her side.

They followed the local custom of dining early, at six, after which they would sit on the verandah to watch the sun set, then retire to bed for a long session of lovemaking. Boy kept them cool by pulling the cord of the punkah, a large flat fan suspended over their bed, with strict instructions not to peep. Peeping was easy in theory, because they kept the windows wide open to catch the sea breeze, but of course, any cessation in the rhythmic swaying of the fan would give him away.

The major found that making love in a tropical country is a whole new experience. Their bodies were covered with a fine dew of moisture even before they began, and as their exertions increased, so they sweated more until it was like massaging each other in oil. The slipperiness made them both more adventurous, and they slithered into positions that surprised and delighted them both (and fascinated Boy, who was able to work the Punkah with his big toe, while seeing into the bedroom with piece of broken mirror).

"Massage me with those!" cried Arthur, gazing at her beautifully shaped breasts. And she did. Ah! what a delight it was to feel, sometimes the softness of the breast and sometimes the rasp of the nipple, She massaged his face – he loved that! She rubbed them over his chest, and was herself delighted by the tickling sensation of his chest hair. She worked lower and pressed a nipple into his navel, and lower still, giving him what his messmates called "a boob job". That was his favourite, especially when combined with what his messmates called "a blow job". It was not just the physical sensation, but the visual delight of seeing his rearing ramrod pressed between those ripe globes, and then the ruby lips open wide to take it in and try to swallow it.

He repaid her by rubbing his ramrod all over her, first while she lay on her back, and then while she lay on her belly. This time, however, he couldn't resist the temptation to slip it in to the welcoming wetness, and to work it hard. Unlike her husband, he had no desire for children, and neither had she, so he pulled it out at the last moment, and delighted Boy with the strongest fountain of youth that he had ever seen. The first squirt went all the way to her neck, the second to the middle of her back, and third, dangerously close to where he had just pulled out.

By now they were soaking with sweat, and Boy knew that, for the next half and hour, he would have to pull at the punkah harder than ever to cool them down. As he fanned them, they lay in each others arms, enjoying the after-sex glow; and after a while, they fell asleep to the music of the Bermuda night – the soothing chorus of the tree frogs.

THE GOVERNOR'S RECEPTION was the high point of their first month on the island. Cassandra had hoped to have a gown made specially for the occasion, as she declared that the gowns she had brought with her were "creased to death". However, she soon found that fashions in Bermuda were even more behind the times than those in York, and decided that it would be better to get the creases out of one of her old gowns. Arthur felt naked out of uniform, but there was nothing he could do about that, except order a civilian outfit with a military cut.

The governor, Sir James Cockburn, and his wife, Lady Augusta Ayscough, welcomed the arrivals. Sir James was dressed in his governor's white uniform with gold epaulettes, and a broad gold-embroidered belt, with a gold-hilted Mameluke Sword suspended from it. Lady Augusta wore a locally-made gown, which, though old-fashioned by London standards, was impressive because of the quality of the silk fabric it was made from. Cassandra, as Mrs Thorpe, had no title to proclaim her status, she therefore attempted to do it by other means, in the shape of a dazzling display of her most expensive jewels.

White uniformed footmen served Champagne to the guests as they gathered in the reception hall. Wealthy expatriates were a rare commodity, and the couple soon found themselves surrounded by numerous people desirous of making their acquaintance. Arthur was particularly impressed by Sir Richard Fitzpatrick who was the colonel of the Bermuda Garrison, currently manned by a detachment of the 47th Foot. At 65, he was a much older man, due to take retirement, but he felt immediately that they had much in common. Moreover, he saw him as a useful acquaintance who could help him to get back into the military. Their first meeting was not a suitable time to raise the matter, but he was confident that the time would come.

Cassandra was charmed by the attention she received from the ladies, and delighted to note that not one of them had a gown that even came close to hers in terms of style. Even more charming was the attention paid to her by the gentlemen. If new expatriates were a rarity, beautiful female expatriates were rarer still.

Of course, they were asked lots of questions, most of them merely innocent topics of conversation, but some of them probing, with the intention of finding out exactly where they might be placed in the social hierarchy. They had expected this, and had prepared a story. They were recently married (and, of course, Cassandra had both an engagement and a wedding ring of the very finest quality) and this was their honeymoon tour. They were *en route* to Barbados, where they planned to visit Cassandra's brother who owned a Sugar Cane Plantation. This was not so wide of the mark, as she did have a distant cousin there. They had taken ship to Bermuda as the first leg of their voyage, and had been so enchanted with the island that they had decided to stay there for a while. All this was accepted without question, and the sugar cane plantation, along with the jewellery around Cassandra's neck, placed them in the category of wealthy upper-class expatriates.

The next part of the evening was dinner in the formal dining room, which Cassandra noted with a pang, was barely half the size of the one at Dale House. The food was excellent, being a combination of Bermuda specialties, such as Fish Chowder and Spiny Lobster with the usual European fare. The wine, which was of the finest quality, was said to have been captured from a French merchant ship.

When the ladies retired, Arthur found himself in conversation with one of the officers of the 47th Foot by the name of Harfield. He was a seedy-looking sort of man, with a long nose and long side whiskers. His hair was streaked with grey which showed him to be rather old for his rank of captain, possibly because he could not afford the purchase of major's commission, but more probably because he had not received the necessary recommendation.

"I say, Cawthorpe," he said, becoming confidential over a glass of Port. "You have the look of a military man about you. Have you ever served, at all?"

Arthur should have said that he hadn't, but he couldn't resist laying claim to military fraternity.

"I was a cornet in the York Militia – but that was a long time ago."

Arthur thought that that should be safe enough. York was a long way from Leeds, and a cornet was a long way from a major.

"Ah, I thought so!" said Captain Harfield. "Always tell a military man. Something about his bearing: upright, proud, fearless – that sort of thing."

He was probably thinking of his own reflection in the mirror as he said this, for he was a rather self-important sort of man, despite his lack of promotion.

Cawthorpe was glad he had requested a military style when ordering his new suit of clothes, because it had already helped him to get to know the right kind of people.

"Tell you what, Cawthorpe," continued the captain. "Wednesday is guest night at the mess. Invitation only, of course. But there's a couple of fellows I'd like you to meet. Shall we say next Wednesday?"

Cawthorpe accepted and was more pleased by the invitation than if he had been invited to sail on the governor's yacht.

Cassandra was also making good progress, for she had made friends with a select clique of women who were known to the young men as "the beauties of Bermuda". They were all married women, but not above a flirtation with the young men. They saw themselves as giving the young men what they called "an emotional education" which would help them when then began a serious courtship. It was self-delusion, of course. All they really wanted was the thrill of flirtation and the satisfaction of a conquest.

When the gentlemen rejoined the ladies, the young men made a bee-line for this group, and Cassandra found herself the object of a thousand flattering attentions – all innocent dalliance, of course, but flattering to her ego. She received numerous invitations to make morning calls, and felt that her social life in Bermuda had begun at last.

Arthur was content to leave the young men to entertain her while he improved his acquaintance with Captain Harfield and two of his friends over a game of whisk for low stakes.

The evening had been a success, and both of them retired to Britney feeling quite delighted with their new country.

The Juliet Trap

Schoolgirls ravished, church collections robbed, clergymen left naked at the side of the road, nothing sacred, nobody safe – these were the rumours that did the rounds – all exaggerated, of course, but not without a degree of truth, and that was why a delegation set out for Carlton Barracks to petition the colonel to do something about it. He immediately looked up Cawthorpe's replacement, Major Wilkinson, and told him to "see to it".

Major Wilkinson sent for Lieutenant Jenkins and discussed tactics.

"What was that plan old Cawthorpe was hatching, do you remember?"

Jenkins scratched his head and tried to remember.

"He called it 'The Juliet Trap', I think, something about a carriage with a balcony."

The major laughed.

"Yes, I remember now. He was only joking about the balcony, of course. He believed that the Romeo of the Road had an informer, so if he put it about that some tasty package (girl plus gold) would be travelling along a certain road at a certain time, he could lay in wait."

"It might work."

"Very well. Let's plan the details, and as soon as we have done that, you can put the word around."

IT WAS A FINE, MOONLIGHT night, the kind of night that made The Romeo of the Road feel nervous and Riff Raff to prefer the safety of the Inn. Nevertheless, the prize was too good to miss, so they ventured out with extra special care. They knew the place well, it was that lonely wooded spot near Bramham, but that was another reason to be careful. The authorities knew about it too.

They waited under cover of the trees until the carriage came into view, then, when it was only about 50 yards away, Romeo rode it in front of it with his pistol held out before him. Meanwhile, Riff Raff covered the carriage from the wood to prevent any attempt by the guard or driver to fight back. In short, if they presented a weapon, Riff Raff would shoot them.

"Stand and Deliver!" called Romeo.

The carriage pulled up, and a moment later, the guard raised his blunderbuss. Riff Raff fired a warning shot.

"Throw it down!" cried Romeo, "or the next shot will be through your head!"

The guard did as he was told, and Romeo rode cautiously up to the carriage, dismounted, and opened the door. Inside were four ladies. It was hard to see whether they were young or old in the darkness, but the glint of their jewellery hinted that this would be as a good a haul as he expected.

"Have no fear," he said. "For The Romeo of the Road never disobliges a lady. Indeed, I am lucky tonight, for we have more than enough to make up a proper square for a Cotillion, and if you will do me the honour, I will spare you your jewellery and only take half your cash."

"Ah'll give yer Cotillion!" growled a rough and very masculine voice, and suddenly the four ladies discarded their cloaks to reveal – four burly troopers. They leapt at him like lions on their prey. He fired his pistol into the air as warning, but it had no effect, and before he could pull his other pistol from his belt, they were on him, punching and kicking, and trying to get him in an arm lock. At the same time, pistol shots were heard in the wood, followed by the sound of galloping hooves on the road. It sounded as though Riff Raff had been attacked, but had managed to get away – he could expect no help from that quarter. One trooper got him in an arm lock, and another pulled the pistol from his belt. "Got 'im!" shouted the third. "Nah tie 'im up!"

A rope was produced and passed around him. It was all up now. He was taken. His only consolation was that he had never killed anybody, so he would probably get off with transportation, though that was punishment enough. Just when he had given up hope, the sound of hooves got louder again, then a shot was fired, and one of his captors slumped to the ground. The others backed off, took cover and returned fire.

It was Riff Raff. He galloped in close, shouted, "Gi' me yer 'and!" and tried to haul Romeo over the croup of his horse. He didn't quite succeed, but he did manage to drag him away from the soldiers. A hail of shot followed them and Romeo felt a sudden impact on his right thigh, though he felt no pain at the time. At almost the same moment, Riff Raff toppled from the saddle.

Romeo tried to bring the horse to a halt, but it had been startled by the gunfire, and was bolting. He clung onto the cantle of the saddle for all he was worth, and might have scrambled into the seat had it not been for the wound in his leg. As it was, he felt his grip weakening, and a moment later, he too, fell into the dust and dirt. Some instinct told him to roll with the momentum of his fall and he dropped into the roadside ditch just as two cavalrymen thundered past in hot pursuit. He knew that they would catch up with the horse in a mile or so, find out that it was riderless, and come back to look for him. He had to get away somehow.

The pain in his thigh was excruciating now. He felt the wound to see how bad it was, and found that blood was everywhere. He took off his scarf and tied it as tightly as he could bear around his thigh, then tried to stand up. He couldn't, because the leg wouldn't bear any weight. So he crawled instead. He crawled into the wood and was tempted to lay there under cover of the trees, but he knew that they would search there, too. He had to keep going until he found a place of safety. The wood seemed endless, and he had to rest every few hundred yards. How tempting it was just to lie there and sleep! – but he knew he must struggle on. At last he came into open country, and saw the silhouette of a small farm not far away. If only he could make it to the barn! But there was a wall in his way, one of the dry-stone walls typical of the region. He looked along it in both directions, and noticed a wicket gate. He crawled towards it, pushed it open, then crawled through into the farmyard. Dogs barked, and he feared they would wake the occupants of the house at any moment, or that they would race up to him, and worry him with their teeth. But nothing happened, and bit by bit, he eased himself across the farmyard and into a barn, the door of which stood wide open as it was used for storing hay rather than livestock. He burrowed into the hay and, safe at last, allowed himself to sink into restful oblivion.

IT WAS THREE IN THE morning by the time the six cavalrymen made it back to Carlton Barracks, four of them on horseback (two of them riding the stray horses) and two of them in the carriage, one of them wounded in the shoulder. There was another body there, that of Riff Raff, who had been shot in the back before he fell from his horse.

"Well done, lads," said Major Wilkinson, "Pity it was such bloody work, though. As for this man..." he nodded towards the body of Riff Raff, "I expect he prefers the bullet to Australia. Anyway, I'm all done in, and I suppose you are too."

There were grunts of agreement.

"Let's get Stevens to the Infirmary, and then turn in. Report to me after Reveille, and we'll make our report to the colonel."

"SO ROMEO GOT AWAY, did he?" said the colonel. "Well, to be honest, I wasn't convinced that such a wild plan would catch anybody. Juliet on a balcony, eh? Funny Juliets! Funny balcony! But it did the trick, and if you'd have looked sharp, you might have got them both. Never mind, one is enough to satisfy public opinion. How is Stevens by the way?"

"Doing well, sir," said Jenkins. "Sitting up in bed with his arm in a sling."

"Good. I'm glad to hear it. What about the dead man?"

"We're going to round up some locals to see if they can identify the body. It's a long shot, but you never know. Burial on Wednesday."

Then, the colonel turned his attention to more important matters:

"Now, about the musket drill..."

Living in Sin

"One can live as well in Bermuda on £1,000 as one can in England on £10,000."

It was Cassandra who said it, and she had meant it as a positive statement. It was not strictly true, because everything in Bermuda had to be imported, and was sold at a premium, but life was simpler and slower. What she was saying, in effect, was that her £10,000 was as good as a £100,000. Arthur, however, saw it differently. Bermuda was all well and good, but there was nothing to spend one's money on. He had bought a horse and gig, though the horse was not what he, a former officer of Hussars, would call a horse. It was, like most of its kind on Bermuda, around 14 hands, a pony, really. As for the gig, it was a far cry from the borrowed curricle he had driven in Leeds – and in any case, where was there to go? The island was only 20 square miles in extent, and most of his regular journeys were only a mile or two – hardly worth the trouble of harnessing the horse (well, pony).

For a while, Wednesday night in the mess provided a satisfying source of entertainment. He was able to hobnob with military men, and later in the evening he would play whisk for high stakes with Captain Harfield and his cronies, Lieutenant Harrison and Ensign Evans. At first it was just as thrilling as play for high stakes at Carlton Barracks. There was the excitement of the game, the ecstasy of winning, and the blood-chilling horror of losing; and the higher the stakes, the more heightened these emotions were. But that soon palled. Even Harfield, who was heir to a small estate in Shropshire, could only play so high, and he was held back by the much more limited means of Harrison and Evans. Losing to the tune of a hundred guineas might have been reason enough for Evans to blow his brains out, but for Arthur, it was a drop in the ocean of that unspendable £10,000. Winning was an even emptier experience, since it only gave him more money that he didn't know what to do with.

In the end, he concluded that the only thing he could do to keep his sanity was to try for that commission in the Bermuda Garrison. So one day he approached Sir Richard to see if it could be arranged.

The colonel stroked his beard as he considered the matter. He was reflecting that Mr Thorpe would have to start with a junior rank, and that he was rather old to be a subaltern. On the other hand, recruits were not easy to get in such remote posting. At last, he said, "As you have no military experience, it could only be as an ensign, and you would have to train with the rank and file until you learn about drill."

Arthur was horrified at the spectacle he would create in front of his new friends, Harfield and the others – especially after all the boasting he had done when he was in his cups. He decided to come clean.

"I have experience up to the rank of major."

The colonel smiled.

"That makes all the difference. Why did not you tell me before?"

Arthur coughed and shuffled in his chair. He was not sure if he was doing the right thing, but he had begun, so he might as well go on.

"There was an incident concerning a lady..."

"Ah..." said the colonel, with a note of reserve, but he was a man of the world, and prepared to see it in perspective.

"But that's not why I was cashiered."

"You were cashiered?"

"I went AWOL, and I had unpaid debts."

"Debts!" repeated the colonel, in the same tone of voice he might have used if Cawthorpe had confessed to murder.

"But – I can afford to pay them now. How would it be if I cleared my debts? Would you consider me for a commission?"

"But – AWOL."

"There were extenuating circumstances, and anyway, AWOL is not desertion."

Sir Richard considered the matter, but it didn't take him long to come to a decision.

"I will write to your colonel. What was the regiment, by the way?"

"18th Hussars, Carlton Barracks, Leeds."

"If he confirms what you say, I see no reason why you should not join us. Indeed, a lieutenant's commission will be available next month, and if you give satisfactory service, I see no reason why you should be a major again in a year's time. An officer's private life is his own business, but as a gentleman, he must pay his debts of honour – not to mention his mess bill – hahaha!"

Arthur was over the moon. A letter to Leeds, and he would be a military man again. Then the emptiness of his present life would be a thing of the past. He could settle down into the old groove and feel that he was a real man instead of a mere lapdog.

ON THE STRENGTH OF his probable commission, Arthur was accepted as a regular in the mess, and it was not long before he was spending almost every evening there. Cassandra saw that it made him happy, and told herself that she should be grateful. She knew that he had gone through another 'dark night of the soul' when he had discovered the limitations of the island, and surely this was better than his giving up and going back to England. That was a disgrace she could never face! But after a month of it, she could bear it no longer.

"Darling!" said sighed. "I thought we came here to be together."

"We are together!"

"I mean – all the time."

"Don't be foolish, darling, no married couples spend all their time together."

"But we don't spend *any* time together, and you never take me anywhere."

He gave a cynical laugh.

"That's because there's nowhere to go. The nearest civilised city is Boston, and that's three day's sailing – not to mention the fact that we're at war with America!"

"I mean here!"

"We went to Sir Richard's only the other evening."

"And you spent all your time talking about flintlocks and foraging while I had to put up with Lady Fitzpatrick who is a crashing bore! She is so out of touch with the fashionable world that she thinks a Grecian is a man from Greece, instead of a new hairstyle, and I had to sit and listen to her and Mrs Dawson gossiping about Bermuda people whom I didn't know, and don't want to know, if what they were saying is true!"

"You will know them soon enough, dear. Then you can join in."

"That's not the point! I thought we came here to be lovers."

"We are lovers. Did we not make love last night – and this morning!"

"Sex is not love! I'm talking about – that feeling – here, in my heart!"

She patted her breast.

Arthur sighed. Why did women want to possess a man so? Why could they not live and let live, like a good friend?

"I'll tell you what it is," he said, "you need something to do. Take myself, for example, I was as miserable as a booby until I got the chance of that commission. Why don't you..." but he couldn't think of anything. It was time to escape.

"Well, I must be off."

"Where are you going?"

"To the mess, of course."

"Can't you spend an evening with me, for once?"

"And do what?"

"We could sit on the verandah, with a glass of Spanish wine, and watch the moon rise. Wouldn't that be romantic!"

Romantic tosh! is what Arthur thought, but he dared not say it. He didn't want to upset her – especially as he would have to ask her to settle his mess bill at the end of the month.

"I'll tell you what. On Sunday, we'll take *Mermaid* out to that little island in the Great Sound and have a picnic."

(*Mermaid* was that yacht he had dreamed about when he first saw the steps down to the jetty).

"Yes, let's," said Cassandra with a happy smile. "That would be wonderful."

Crisis over, thought Arthur – for now.

Confessions in a Barn

Romeo was awakened by a gentle touch on his face. He opened his eyes and saw two green eyes staring into his. He recognised them immediately as Dolly's. He tried to sit up, but an excruciating pain ripped down the right side of his body. He groaned and lay back.

"Don't try ter move," she said. "You're 'urt. There's blood everywhere. Let me see."

She examined his leg, found the tourniquet and took it off. Luckily for Romeo it had worked loose during the night, or he might have lost his leg.

"Tek your breeches off so's ah can get a proper look."

But he could barely move, let alone take his breeches off.

"Ah'll have to cut 'em off. Wait. Ah'll be back."

She returned with a large pair of scissors and gently cut his breeches just above the wound. Then she examined it closely.

"It looks like t' ball 'as winged yer an' taken off a chunk o' flesh. It needs to be cleaned an' stitched. Ah'll send for a doctor."

Romeo grabbed her arm. "No!" he said, urgently.

"But you must! If that wound gets infected you could lose yer leg!"

"I can't risk it."

"Why?"

Romeo was silent, but Dolly answered for him.

"Ah know why. Ah know who yer are."

His heart missed a beat.

"Yer *'im*, aren't yer?" she continued.

He affected not to understand.

"Who?"

But it was no good.

"The Romeo o' t' Road, that's who!"

He heaved a sigh. Well, at least his leg would get proper attention, even if it meant going to Australia.

"But don't worry," she said brightly. "Ah won't turn yer in."

"You won't?" he said, surprised. "Why not?"

"Because yer treated me well – remember? When yer 'eld me up. Yer didn't tek me churns, an' yer gave me a guinea for a shillin', an'..."

There was something else, but she didn't know how to put it.

"And?" he prompted.

"Ah've never heard any bad on yer. You tek the money, but yer never h'urt anybody – not like that ovver gang. Just imagine! Ravishing schoolgirls, leaving as poor parson naked in the road!"

Romeo felt that he should put matters straight.

"That incident of the schoolgirls..."

But Dolly interrupted.

"Terrible, weren't it? Every one o' 'em stripped and ravished! But you wouldn't do a thing like that cos you're a gentleman."

She hesitated.

"But why do yer do it at all?"

"It's a long story," he said with a groan.

The groan reminded her of his wound.

"Ah'd better fix yer up," she said. "You can tell me yer story later. 'Ang on a mo', ah'm guin' ter fetch some stuff."

"And bring me a drink – I'm dying of thirst!"

She was back a moment later with a bottle of water, and a basket of medical supplies.

"First ah've got ter clean t' wound, an' ah've got ter be thorough. It'll 'urt, so tek this."

She gave him a bottle of whiskey. He took a gulp, then braced himself. She had brought a bottle of vinegar, and poured some of it onto a cloth, then tentatively touched the wound. He howled.

"That's no good! Yer'll 'ave Molly an' Matt pokin' their noses in. 'Ere, bite on this."

She gave him a leather thong. Romeo took another swig of whiskey and bit. Then she started to rub. He bit the thong, screamed (though more quietly because of the thong in his mouth) and writhed.

"Keep still!"

He did – because he had passed out.

When he came to, she was bandaging the wound.

"There!" she said. "All done! Ah've cleaned it, stitched it an' bandaged it."

"You stitched it?"

"Yes."

Their eyes met. His blue looked into her green with a new respect.

"How come you know how to stitch a wound?"

"A Dalesman's daughter knows a lot of stuff that yer'd never dream on. What do yer think, that we send for the vet ev'ry time a cow cuts hersel' on a broken fence? Now, ah'm goin' ter bring yer a pillow an' some blankets, an' mek yer comfortable. Ah daren't move yer yet, but you'll be all reet 'ere for now. Ah'll 'ave ter cover you wi' hay, though."

She disappeared for a while, then came back with pillow and blankets, and tucked him up like a child.

"Now try an' get some sleep. Yer'll hear t' cows comin' in later on, but tek no notice. Me an' Molly'll be milkin' 'em, but she'll not know yer there if yer keep quiet."

Robin slept for the rest of the morning. He was dimly aware of the lowing of cows, and the chatter of Dolly and Molly, but more than anything else of the painful throbbing in his thigh.

It was late afternoon when she woke him with a bottle of warm tea and a chicken sandwich. He ate and drank greedily, then lay back.

"How d'yer feel now?" said Dolly, regarding him intently.

"Better," he said, then tried to move, and groaned aloud.

"You still need to rest," she said. "Ah've brought some more blankets ter keep yer warm. It's gettin' cold of a night."

Robin looked at her closely, and liked what he saw.

"*You* can keep me warm. Lie down beside me."

"Ah don't mind if ah do," she said, "because ah know there can be no funny business wi' that leg of yourn."

She lay down at his side, but kept at a safe distance, just out of arm's reach.

"Now then," she said. "Yer can tell me yer story."

"I'd rather hear yours."

She gave him a surprised look.

"Mine? What's interesting about a dalesman's daughter's life. It's just sheep an' cows, an' sheep an' cows, an' a few chicken thrown in – like that un yer eatin' now."

Robin stopped eating and looked at his sandwich. The thought that he was eating a creature that had been strutting round the farmyard that very morning was something of a novelty.

"But surely, a girl as beautiful as you must have a sweetheart."

"Thank you, kind sir," she said archly, trying to remember when she had heard those words before. "You must be gettin' better if you can think o' flattery."

"Well?"

"Not one."

"Not Fred Figget?"

She sat up suddenly. "'Ow do you know about Fred Figget?"

Robin wondered if he had given himself away, but then an obvious retort came to mind.

"I have spies everywhere."

"Anyway, Fred Figget is not for me. Ah want summat better."

"Such as?"

"A duke."

Robin gave an uneasy laugh. "What makes you think a duke would want you?"

"Ah danced wi' Lord Linton once. 'Ee seemed to like me."

"There's a big difference between liking and marrying. Anyway, Lord Linton is married. Why don't you set your sights a little lower – a gentleman farmer, perhaps."

"Like my da?"

"Why not? Mr Dalton looks every bit the gentleman in his Sunday best."

Dolly frowned as she tried to put her feelings into words.

"Because... because... I don't know. Tell me your story, it might help me to explain what I mean."

"I'm a gentleman by birth..."

"Ah can tell, by yer voice."

"And I have a competency..."

"Ah guessed."

"But I wanted to do something for the poor folk of Wharfedale. It's hard life..."

"Ah know."

Robin looked hard into those great green eyes. "Do you want to hear my story, or not?"

"O' course ah do."

"Then listen like a good girl, and stop interrupting. They work until they are too old to work, then if there is nobody to look after them, they end up in the almshouse, or worse, begging on the streets. I did what I could – I won't go into that now – but I was horrified that most rich people do nothing at all, and so, to cut a long story short, I took to the road. You know the rest, because I told you when I held you up."

"But if yer have a – what d'yer call it – a competency – that means money, don't it?"

"Yes, a private income from – some land I own."

"Well, yer can give the poor folk some o' that.

"I can and I do, but there's another reason I took to the road – a disappointment in love. But I don't want to talk about that..."

"Ooh, do!"

"No, it's too personal."

Dolly shuffled closer towards him and looked deeply into his eyes to try to divine his secret.

"Go on – a love story's much more interestin' than 'ighway robbery!"

"No."

"Ah'll tell yer about me an' Fred if yer do."

"Later, perhaps, but first let me finish my story."

"Go on, then."

"After a while, it became so bad that certain ladies put themselves in the way of being held up."

"Why would they do that?"

"Perhaps because they wanted to spice up their dull lives with excitement, adventure and romance."

Dolly came closer, her green eyes wide with sudden understanding.

"That's it! You've said t' words ah wa' strugglin' fer: excitement, adventure an' romance! Fred Figgit is a good, solid chap, but 'ee's as dull as ditchwater. Ah should die o' boredom if wa' married to 'im!"

"Perhaps a duke's life is boring," suggested Robin.

Dolly stuck out her determined chin.

"Well it shou'n't be!" she said with decision. "A duke 'as money, 'igh connections, an' power – so 'ee's only 'imself to blame if 'is life is borin' – an' if it is, well, 'ee's a... 'ee's a..." Dolly was stuck for a word. She looked around and noticed the ragwort straggling round the door post, "...weed!" she concluded with emphasis.

Robin groaned. It might have been because he thought the insult was aimed at him, but more probably because his leg was uncomfortable.

"I've told you my story. Now tell me about Fred."

"There' nothin' to tell. You tell me about yer disappointment in love."

"If you tell me about Fred."

"Like ah said, there's nothin' ter tell. But what there is ah'll tell it, so's ah can 'ear yer story."

She collected her thoughts, took a deep breath, and began. "Fred wants to marry me, an' pa wants 'im ter marry me..."

"And you don't want to marry him, is that it?"

"Ah told yer ah didn't!"

"Do you remember the Race Week Barn Dance?"

Dolly looked at him strangely.

"'Ow do you know about that? Was you there?"

"I told you, I have spies."

"Hmm, well, Fred proposed to me at t' dance, an' ah told 'im ter get lost – in a nice sort o' way, o' course..."

"There's no nice way to turn a man down."

Dolly looked hard into those enigmatic blue eyes.

"Do yer want to hear me story, or not?"

"Of course I do."

"Then listen like a good boy, an' don't interrupt. Pa was so mad that 'ee sent me away. That's why ah'm 'ere. This is me aunt's farm, an' ah'm to stay 'ere, workin', until ah 'come to me senses' – as Pa puts it. That's it. Nah tell me your love story."

Robin sighed.

"It's a common tale of married life, I'm afraid. My marriage was arranged for reasons of property and title. I liked the woman, and I hoped we would grow to love each other. But she never seemed satisfied. She took no interest in my work – the estate, the tenants, the common good – and thought only of herself. I tried to win her, but the more I tried, the more I seemed to drive her away. She was unfaithful, I know, and in the end she... but I must say no more."

Dolly was devouring his every word, indeed, she was so close that she was almost devouring him. Her mane of red-gold hair hung around his head, and he could feel her hot breath in his face.

"Oh you poor thing!" she sighed, "but do go on!"

"I mustn't."

"Well then, ah think she ran away wi' him."

Robin pursed his lips, determined to say nothing.

"Oh you poor boy!" said Dolly with a gush of emotion so strong that it caused her to kiss him. It was more a kiss of sympathy than anything else, but Robin liked it, put his arm round her neck, and wouldn't let her pull away. They kissed fully and frankly for a few moments, and he stroked her magnificent mane, and would have stroked elsewhere, but Dolly, conscious of her position, drew back, rolled over, and stood up. She brushed the hay from her dress, smoothed her tangled locks with her hand, and became suddenly matter-of-fact.

"Ah must think o' a plan. Yer can't stay 'ere forever, yer know," and with those words she left him. He had a throbbing pain in his leg, but the tingling sensation on his lips made him forget all about it.

If it Ain't Black

Captain Harfield was a bad influence. When he was not gambling or drinking, he was chasing women. Sometimes it was the Irish whores who hung around the hulks, and at others it was the black whores who hung around the bars of Hamilton. Every now and then he might get lucky with the bored wife of a long-term expatriate, but they were few and far between.

He was holding forth on his conquests one evening, over a glass (or several) of claret.

"When I first came to Bermuda, I went for the Irish girls. The prisoners in the hulks are, by and large Irish, and in some cases, their families come over to be near them. They live in a shanty settlement on the North Shore, and, believe me, they are dirt poor. Well, the daughters can get a few shillings by offering up the booty (as we say here). Then I began to notice the black girls, and one type in particular: the Black Caribs. Little beauties, they are. Fine-boned, like Asians. Long black hair, big black eyes, and big... well, you know what I mean. Now I know what the Bermuda veterans mean when they say: 'If it ain't black, send it back.'"

The idea was a revelation to Cawthorpe, because he had not thought of black women in that way at all. Indeed, he had not thought of them in any way. Just like the Dalesfolk where he came from, they did all the necessary work in the world so that he could enjoy himself, and that was all.

The result of that conversation was that, next morning, he looked at Abigail for the first time, and found that she was exactly as Harfield had said. She had fine-boned, delicate features, and long black hair that fell down her back almost to her waist. Her eyes were black, too, and seemed all the more eloquent because of the contrast of the whites to her black skin, and though she was only fifteen, her breasts were full and round. Her posterior had the same well-rounded quality.

It was her custom to get washed under the pump as soon as she got up. Usually, this was in the middle of Arthur's beauty sleep, but he had got up that morning especially to watch her. She was modest about her wash, keeping her shift on all the time and washing herself around it, but as she had no thought of being observed, there were plenty of flashes of bare flesh, and in any case the water made the shift transparent.

Arthur was transfixed. Here was a veritable beauty right under his nose, and he had never noticed her. Every morning she gave a more alluring performance under that pump than ever he had seen at *The Pussycat Theatre* in London. And the best of it was that she was all his – she was not a slave, of course, because Slave Trading had been made illegal in Bermuda in 1807, but he knew well that she would be delighted to satisfy his every need for a shilling.

Arthur put his hand in his left pocket to feel for a shilling and in his right pocket to feel for something else which he intended to rub up and down, but just then, Cassandra came in.

"What are you looking at with such interest?" she said.

"Oh, nothing," he said, with affected nonchalance. "I was just going to close the shutter."

LATER, CASSANDRA WENT to make one of her morning calls, and Arthur decided to take advantage of the opportunity. He rang the bell and Abigail appeared. She made a cute little courtesy and said, "Wah mi can duh fi yuh, sah?"

Arthur looked her appreciatively up and down and said, "Take your clothes off."

She did, as naturally and unselfconsciously as she would have brought him a cup of tea.

"Now come here."

She did, and he began to stroke her all over. Ah! The thrill of young, firm flesh! Then he kissed her. First on the lips, then on her pert breasts, then on he bellybutton and then on her *mons*, discovering, as he did so that she was deliciously pink inside.

He picked her up (she was quite small and light) carried her into the bedroom, and threw her on the quasi-conjugal bed, Then he jumped on top of her and began the exercise that he loved. She welcomed him with open legs, which she wrapped around him with evident enthusiasm. Her moves seemed practised, and it was clear that this was not the first time she had offered up the booty (no wonder Boy had such a broad smile on his face). She wriggled and writhed like a young animal and seemed to be enjoying herself. What a sight it was to see that black body on his! It was the contrast that was so delicious. Arthur was no poet, but the beautiful sight made him poetic: ebony and ivory, like keys on piano keyboard, side by side in perfect harmony! Yes, something like that could be made into a poem or a song – but not now, he had other things to do. He turned her over and put her on top, the better to enjoy the tantalising sight – and that was when Cassandra came into the bedroom.

"Arthur! Where are you? I..."

There was a moment of horrified silence followed by an ear-splitting scream, In a moment the whole household was peering round the doorway, Abe, Bertha and Boy, thinking that the house was about to fall down – and there was Arthur, on his back, with Abigail on top of him.

"I'm leaving!" cried Cassandra, and stormed out of the house.

"Get back to your work," Arthur said to the staff, while thinking, "and I'll get back to mine."

He put Abigail on her knees, and worked her until he achieved his final fantasy – to see a splattering of his white sperm on her black skin. He sighed, "Ebony and ivory," again and rolled off her.

He lay for a while contemplating the punkah, which boy, so thoughtfully, had started working, then suddenly, the full horror of what had just happened hit him like a punch from a prizefighter. He sat up with a jolt and said out loud: "Egad! I've done it now!" and it couldn't have been at a worse time, for his mess bill was due in a few days.

IT WAS A THE LOW-WATER mark of their relationship. When she came back he tried to persuade her that it meant nothing.

"It was only a bit of fun."

"You showed me up before our entire household!"

"You, yourself said, 'sex is not love', and that's all it was – sex."

"You should save yourself for me!"

He almost said that he had enough for her and half a dozen Abigails, but realised that she would misinterpret it and think that he wanted an orgy.

"Anyway, I promise that I will not do it again, and you know that an officer's word is his bond."

"I know what military men are like. What you said only applies to affairs of honour, such as gambling debts, not to women."

Arthur saw his cue and decided that an early retreat was in order.

"Which reminds me that I promised Harfield a game of whisk this afternoon, so if you'll excuse me."

She became hysterical again.

"That's it, go! Leave me alone like you always do!"

He did.

THAT NIGHT CASSANDRA slept in another bedroom – not that Arthur noticed, for he came back from the mess very late and very drunk – so drunk, in fact, that he got up too late to witness the show under the pump which he had described to his messmates with so much relish that Evans had said, "I'd like to see that!"

Harrison had responded in all seriousness by suggesting that they set up a pump in the mess and charged a guinea a head for the show, but Cawthorpe thought of a simpler solution: "Just come round any morning at six and you can see it for free."

"Six! I don't get to bed until four!"

"It's worth it, I can assure you."

"I'll tell you what, I'll give you a guinea, and her a shilling, and she can take a wash in my quarters, and come to bed with me after."

Cawthorpe shook his head.

"She's mine. I've only just discovered her and I intend to make the most of her – when..."

He was going to say, "When the storm has died down," but a military man never admits to trouble with his better half.

As it happened, there was no show under the pump that morning, and there never would be again, because as soon as Cawthorpe had left for the mess, Cassandra had sent for Abigail and dismissed her, resolving to find the oldest, ugliest and most bad-tempered replacement in Bermuda.

Arthur woke up with a terrible hangover. When he finally managed to drag himself out of bed, he went to the kitchen for a cup of coffee, and was told by Bertha that there was a pot on the table on the verandah where madam was taking breakfast.

He found Cassandra toying with her food and looking disconsolately out to sea. He sat down opposite her and poured himself a cup of coffee. He took several gulps, then rubbed his temples. His hangover was no better.

"I blame that Madeira they serve in the mess," he said, hoping to avoid any mention of the Abigail incident. "It's not from Madeira at all, but some benighted South American country." (Actually, it was the real thing, from the Madeira Islands – he had just drunk too much of it).

She said nothing.

"The Claret's not bad though. They stocked up on it before the French wars. Genuine Bordeaux – smooth as baby's bottom."

She looked away and sipped her tea.

"I won 20 guineas at whisk. Tell, you what, I'll take you out to Tom Moore's tonight. Best restaurant in town, so Harfield says."

She had heard enough of his irrelevant nonsense, and rounded on him.

"Why don't you take Harfield? You think more of him than me," she snapped.

"Harfield is just a messmate!"

It was getting ridiculous. He could understand her being jealous about his little fling with Abigail – but jealous of a friend!

"You don't love me! That's what it is!"

"Of course I love you! I gave up everything to be here!"

"And now you're getting it all back again – the army, cards, drinking – women."

"Of course I want to get back into the army. It's who I am. Can't you see that? Without it, I'm just a..." a stray faggot of wood on the lawn provided him with his analogy: "...piece of driftwood, floating aimlessly here and there, until I'm washed up, desolate, on some remote beach."

"And this is the remote beach," I suppose.

"Not if I can get into the army. I'll be happy then."

"Then you'll spend all your time in the mess, and you'll have to go and fight the Americans, and you'll get killed, and I'll have no choice but to..." she looked out to sea, as if the answer was there "...jump off that cliff!"

Arthur smiled.

"I wouldn't do that dear. It's only 12 feet high and you might get wet."

"It's not funny!"

"Anyway, you don't have to worry about the Americans. We're here to defend the island, it's true, but they've got to get past the Royal Navy first!"

"Oh, why did I leave Robert! He was a good man. I can see it now. I thought he was boring, but he was a man of honour; a man who did his duty. He wouldn't take advantage of a young servant girl! He wouldn't spend night after night drinking with his friends..."

"Come now. He was away a lot."

"Yes, doing his duty, not – revelling!"

"It's a hard life in the army, you know. An officer may have to face death, and so he lives life to the full while he can."

"Robert loved me in his own way, but I was stupid, I wanted excitement, adventure and, above all – romance. I thought I'd found it with you, but..."

"Come, darling, don't take it so hard. You've had excitement – for what can be more exciting than an elopement? And you've had adventure – for what can be more adventurous than crossing the Atlantic to discover an island paradise? And you've had romance – for what can be more romantic than making love with Hussar in the heat of a tropical night while the tree frogs sing outside?"

Arthur saw himself as a man of action, not of words, but the Poet Laureate, Robert Southey, could not have done better. He had made it sound as though she was living a wonderful life, and in the main it was true, and she felt somewhat mollified.

Arthur saw his advantage and attempted to build on it.

"Look, I don't care a jot for other women, and I wouldn't have looked twice at Abigail if she hadn't washed naked under the pump..." (which was not strictly true). It's you I love. As for the mess, I'm doing my best to get a commission, and when I've got it, I need only go there once a week (though he intended to go every night). I'll tell you what, why don't we have a big house party and invite everyone we know, and entertain them, London style? We'll give a party that will be the talk of Bermuda for years to come."

That idea appealed to many of Cassandra's vanities: she would show herself off in a new gown, made from a design in a French fashion magazine; she would show her 'husband' off, resplendent in the scarlet and gold of his new uniform; she would show off her household management, through the most delicious food, produced by the finest cooks in Bermuda; she would hire the Hamilton Chamber Orchestra to provide music for dancing; and to compensate for the lack of space in their villa, she would have an enormous marquee to serve as a ballroom. No expense would be spared, for she was determined that people would talk about her party for years to come, and that it would position her as one of the leading socialites in Bermuda society.

Love in a Haystack

The Bramham farm cock had only just announced daybreak when Dolly appeared with breakfast.

"Yer could do wi' bacon an' eggs, but they'd notice, so ah've brought yer bread an' cheese an' a pint o' small beer."

He tucked into it with a will, and while he was eating she outlined her plan.

"Now, we could do wi' another man on t' farm, and ah'm goin' to suggest you."

Robin laughed.

"What will you say: 'Aunt, here is a highwayman to dig your ditches'?"

She gave him a playful slap.

"No, silly. Ah'll say there's man by the name of Robin – Robin, what?"

"What about 'Hood'?"

She slapped him again.

"Don't be daft. What's yer real name?"

"'Dale' is close enough. Go on."

"Ah'll say that ah know yer, an' that yer've worked for Pa..."

"What if she checks?"

"Pa can't remember t' name o' everybody who's worked for 'im. Ah'm not worried about that. Then she'll set yer on, an' yer can work 'ere until yer feel it's safe ter go. What can yer do?"

Robin considered, and quickly reached a conclusion.

"Nothing. I know about horses, and that's about it."

"Let me look at yer 'ands," she said.

He held them out and she took them, turned them over and stroked his palms.

"They're like a girl's," she said, "soft as…"

He finished the sentence for her: "…your lips," and, keeping hold of her hands, he pulled her towards him to kiss her. She was looking particularly attractive that morning. She was wearing a simple country gown and an apron, but the gown had lacing down the front, and for some reason, by accident or design, perhaps because she was in a hurry, or perhaps because she wanted to display her charms to her guest, she had left the top laces undone. But his leg was still very sore, and he was not very manouvreable. She pushed him away with ease and stood up.

"None o' that!" she said "This is serious. Yer'll have to do some real work or yer'll get found out."

"You could teach me."

"No, Matt'll teach yer. There's one other thing, though."

"What?"

"We can't pass yer off as a farm 'and if yer talkin' all lah-di-dah, like. Yer'll 'ave ter talk like me."

"Teach me."

She smiled.

"Ah'll mek a bargain. Ah'll teach you to talk Daleish if you'll teach me to talk lah-di-dah. Ah can fake it a bit, but ah'd do a lot better wi' some lessons. Ah s'll never be a duchess if ah don't speak proper."

"I thought you were joking about being a duchess."

She gave him an arch look with her green eyes.

"Per'aps ah am, mebbe it's just a way o' sayin' that ah want better'n Fred Figgit."

"It's a deal, then. Let's begin. First you must say every word clearly with the correct pronunciation. Don't say 'ah'll', say "I will", and sound your aitches. Let's try it. Now, say after me: 'In Hertford, Hereford and Hampshire hurricanes hardly ever happen'"

"In 'ertford, 'ereford and 'ampshire 'urricanes 'ardly ever 'appen."

"No, Dolly, take a deep breath and say 'hhhhhh'"

She took a deep breath and that part of her bosom which was visible above the laces, gave an enticing heave. Robin noticed and began to feel aroused.

"Now do that before every word."

"In Hhhhertford, Hhhhereford and Hhhhampshire hhhhurricanes hhhhhardly ever happen."

Her bosom heaved up and down with every word and his body reacted in the way that God had intended when he designed those jewels in the female crown. Robin reached for her again, but a sudden pain prevented him and he lay back with a groan.

It was not a ploy, but if it had been, it could not have been better planned, for in a moment she was leaning over him with her hand round his head, and her beautiful red-gold hair in his face as she kissed his forehead. He strained forward again, the pain in his leg as nothing to the desire in his heart, and this time he managed to plant a kiss between her breasts. For a moment she pressed towards him and revelled in the sensation, then she pulled away, and continued their conversation as if nothing had happened.

"Nah, it's your turn. Yer've got ter drop your aitches an' flatten yer vowels. A good tip is to say 't' really quickly, instead of 'the'. Nah then, try this: 'T' rain in Spain falls mainly on t' plain' – an' mind you flatter yer vowels. So it's not 'Spain' with 'ay' but 'Spehn' with a sort of 'eh' sound. Try it."

"The rehn in Spehn.."

"Not 'the', 't'."

"'T' rehn in Spehn falls mehnly on t'plehn."

"Good! Matt coul'n't 'a' said it better!"

It is quite exciting to hear members of the opposite sex use obscene words, so when Dolly said, or seemed to say, 'cunt', Robin's rod became harder still, and he was inspired to unfasten more of her laces. At the same moment the Bramham farm cock crowed again, and the words 'cock' and 'cunt' were racing around in his brain. But she pushed him away again. With his leg as it was, even the notorious Romeo of the Road was no threat.

"Well, when a girl uses a word like 'cunt', what do you expect?"

She rolled with laughter.

"You're from round these parts, aren't yer? 'Ave yer never 'eard that word before? Yorkshire folks say 'cou'n't' all the time, but they don't mean... well, I canna say t' word."

They both laughed. It was a strange sort of language lesson, but over the next few days they both made good progress, and by the end of the week, Robin's leg was well enough for him to be presented to Aunt Dalton.

"Where are yer from?" was her first question.

"Kirkby Lonsdale."

They had agreed this story to account for any oddities in his accent.

"That's a way away. Cumberland, ain't it?"

"Aye."

"What can yer do?"

"Everythin'..." God forgive me for telling a lie, thought Robin, "Ah can 'erd cows, muck aht t' pigs, dig ditches an' fix fences. Jack o' all work, that's me."

Dolly smiled proudly at her pupil. They had rehearsed this little speech almost as often as he had made her repeat the drill about hurricanes (for the wrong reasons).

"Well, ah can't pay much. Ten shillin' a week is all."

"That will do very nicely, thank you," said Robin, so grateful to be accepted so easily that it came out in his usual 'lah-di'dah' voice. Dolly scowled at him, but Aunt Dalton seemed not to notice.

"Tek 'im to meet Matt, an' Matt'll show 'im what wants doin'," said Aunt Dalton, dismissing the matter, and turning round to rebuke Molly, who was earwigging in the hall when she should have been doing the laundry.

NOW THAT THE LEG WAS better, and the dialect had been mastered (to some extent) there was another matter to attend to, so Robin hung around the barnyard door until Dolly went past.

"Can yer help us," he said, in his best Daleish, "Ah'm havin' a bit o' trouble wi' one o' t' farmyard critters."

"Where?" she said.

"In here," he replied, and led her into the barn.

As soon as she was inside, she looked round in puzzlement at the empty space, and said, "Which critter?"

"A cock!" he declared, grabbing her hand and placing it on his manhood. "It's all swollen up, an' only you can heal it – you know how."

"Ah cou'n't!" she protested.

"Exactly!"

Dolly changed to lah-di-dah-speak to make herself clear.

"No, what I mean is, that I couldn't! I know you're a duke, but it's wrong to take advantage of a poor Dalesman's daughter."

Robin was stunned.

"Who said I was a duke?"

Dolly laughed. "I've known it all along."

"How?"

"Those eyes. Nobody else has eyes like you. Blue as heaven and sometimes soft and sometimes hard."

"Like this!" he said, pressing her hand harder into his groin.

"No!" she said. "I want to be a duchess, not a sex-doll!"

"But I love you!" protested Robert, for that was his real name; the name that had been pronounced when the previous vicar of Dale had made the sign of the cross on his forehead at his Christening, thirty-five years ago.

"I bet you said that to all those ladies in the carriages."

"That's not true. I offered to leave them half their worldly goods for a Cotillion and a kiss. Unfortunately, some of them mistook the word 'kiss' as a synecdoche for a – well, I know you don't like obscene words, but it begins with 'f'."

"I know the 'f'-word, but what is a 'synecdoche' – is it nice, is it rude?"

"Take that gown off and I'll show you – no, I'm only kidding. It's the kind of thing they teach you at Cambridge. It's a figure of speech where the part stands for the whole. What I am trying to say is that those ladies had dull, unfulfilled lives, and they saw me as a chance for – romance, perhaps, or perhaps just a good... kiss (as a synecdoche) – without incurring any disgrace. After all, when a pistol is pointed at your head, you have to give in."

"But you never forced them?"

"Ha! They forced me – well, encouraged me. I was in despair with my love life so I didn't need much encouraging."

"Are you in despair now?"

"No, because I have you."

"But I'm not going to let you have me. I'm saving myself for my duke, in which 'duke' is a synecdoche for a life full of excitement, adventure and romance."

"You're a fast learner. Anyway, there is no need to save yourself, because I am here now. I am your duke."

"You're just trying to get me into the haystack."

"No, I really love you, and I think you love me too."

"How do you know?"

"I've known it all along."

"How?"

"Those eyes. Nobody else has eyes like you. Green as the grass, and open as this barn door. What I mean is, I can read them like a synecdoche. They are a part that stands for the whole, and the whole is you, and that is what I want."

"I'm still not coming in the haystack."

"But you will save yourself for your duke?"

"Yes."

"Then I will go to London and get a divorce."

The green eyes were wide.

"You surely don't mean it!"

"Of course I do, there's just one thing."

"The haystack?"

"No. I want to know that you love me too."

"But you do know, you said you could read it in my eyes."

"Eyes are not as precise as words in a book, or words on lips."

"Lips," she said, and kissed him for a very long time and at the end of the kiss, she said the words, just to be sure: "I love you. Do I need to write it down as well?"

"No."

"What about the haystack?"

"Come on, then."

There is nothing sweeter than freshly-mown hay, and nothing sweeter than a lover's kiss, so they were both transported to heaven, even though heaven was a humble haystack. Another advantage was that they could make love in three dimensions, as though they were in a kind of dense water. Robert lay on top of Dolly and kissed her so intensely, that her head sank into the hay, and soon they were almost upside down in the hay, then, when he entered her, the pressure on her hips brought them round the other way, and soon she was straddling him.

It was Dolly's first time, so she was sore, and bleeding a little, but she didn't mind that, because for her, the pleasure was in her heart, she had her duke, and her duke was a man she loved.

Robert saw the blood and said, "Does it hurt?"

"Yes a little, but I don't mind."

"It will be better next time."

"I was wonderful this time."

They sat up and discovered that they'd spread the haystack over most of the barn floor.

"We've messed up all the hay," she said with a little laugh.

"Never mind, Matt can fork it up again."

"That's your job. You're the new hand."

"Not anymore. I'm the Duke of Linton and I'm going to London to get a divorce."

"You were serious, then, when you said you'd marry me?"

"Yes."

"I thought men always let women down."

"Some do, but not me. But listen. It won't be easy. First I've got to find Major Cawthorpe. I've heard he is in Bermuda, which is lucky, because that's a British colony and British law applies, so I can bring an action against him. But it will have to go through parliament, and will cost a pretty penny. It could also take a long time – years, I'm afraid. Will you wait for me?"

"Of course, I will. I've been waiting for you all my life."

"What about Fred Figget?"

She laughed, "A hundred Fred Figgets are not worth the little finger of my duke!"

A Tropical Storm

Arthur's idea of the grand house party had managed to avert a disaster in his relationship with Cassandra, and several happy weeks followed. He was happy in the expectation of his commission, and she was happy in the business of preparation for the big event.

However, Arthur's attempt to get a commission was to prove their undoing. The letter written by the colonel created a disastrous link between his new life and his old. It told everybody in Yorkshire (for these things will leak out) where he was, and everybody in Bermuda (for with such a small population, everybody knows everything about everybody) that he was not Mr Thorpe, but Mr Cawthorpe, and that Mrs Thorpe was actually Lady Linton, and that worse of all (on a highly religious island) they were living in sin.

The first that they knew of it was when the invitations to the house party were not acknowledged – or not by the great and the good. There are always those people who don't care about the reputation of their hosts, so long as the food is good, and there are always those who like to come along and gloat, but the people that mattered stayed aloof.

Arthur found out the reason when he went to enquire about his commission:

Had the colonel received a reply to his letter?

Yes.

Did it confirm the story he had told him?

Yes.

Could he buy the available commission?

Ah...

The colonel explained that, while the army was not concerned with an officer's private life, it could not sanction an officer living under a false name. Nor was the army concerned about an officer's morality, but it could not turn a blind eye to a single officer cohabiting with a married woman – especially in a small, and deeply Christian, community such as Bermuda. In short, he recommended that Cawthorpe and Lady Linton assumed their proper names and lived separately. Beyond that requirement, the army had no interest in the matter. If he took Lady Linton as his mistress, that was his own concern – though it was expected that any affair would be carried on discreetly. When these conditions were fulfilled, Cawthorpe was welcome to apply for the commission.

The news was both good and bad. On the one hand, after a few domestic adjustments, his commission was assured, on the other, he knew that he would have great difficulty in persuading Cassandra to accept such a reduction in her circumstances.

Arthur was soon to discover that he had grossly underrated her reaction. She screamed, she howled, she had hysterics, she threatened to throw herself off the cliff. It was like one of those tropical storms that ravage Bermuda every year: there's nothing to be done, except hunker down until the storm has blown over.

He tried to fend it off by saying in his most pleading tone: "But, darling, we can still be lovers, and that's all that matters, isn't it?"

He had hoped that the word 'lovers' would act as a palliative, but it only made things worse.

"Am I to live by myself then, shunned by society, while you visit me to take your pleasure? That's a whore, not a lover!"

He tried again: "I thought that…"

But the storm only got worse: "That's just the trouble! You only think about yourself. You weren't content to be a wealthy civilian, were you? Oh no! You had to try to get back into the army, even if it meant giving away all our secrets! And now we're disgraced!"

Arthur said nothing; it would only make matters worse.

"Who am I going to socialise with, now? Street whores?"

Arthur almost referred to the wives of his fellow officers, but bit his lips just in time.

"We can't stay here! And we can't go back to England! There's only one thing for it; we'll go to Barbados and try again."

Arthur didn't like that idea, and couldn't keep his lips buttoned.

"But my commission!"

"Comission! Commission! Commission! It's a pity you can't marry your commission!"

Arthur thought it was a pity, too.

Cassandra calmed down after this rant. Arthur hoped that it had been the final blast of the storm, and it was, because the word 'Barbados', which she had mentioned quite randomly, gave her the solution she was looking for – and it was the ideal solution, for it would satisfy two requirements. Above all, it would enable them to begin again as Mr and Mrs Thorpe, but it would have the added advantage that it would put Arthur to the test. If he really loved her, he would sacrifice his commission and live with her as a civilian.

"So what about Barbados?" she said, pointedly.

Arthur had no intention of going to Barbados, but he didn't want to face another hurricane, so with a smile and a gallant kiss, he said, "What a wonderful idea!" and breathed a sigh of relief.

There is something particularly exciting about sex when making up after a quarrel. The person that you thought you were losing, is yours again. It is almost like new love, and for Arthur and Cassandra it led to another storm; a storm of passion that was the mirror image of their stormy argument. It was a bit like those Bermuda hurricanes, where after the first blow, there is a lull in the 'eye', and then it all happens again.

She wrapped her legs around him and pulled him into her without any foreplay (the argument was the foreplay), then she grabbed his butt cheeks and pulled at them to make his thrusts harder and deeper, all the time, howling with delight, and using language that he had never heard her use before, and never heard anywhere else except in the mess.

Then she ran her nails down his back, drawing blood. The pain was a kind of pleasure, and it inspired him to pay her back. He rolled her over and gave her a sound smacking for her childish jealousy, then, provoked by the red blush on her butt cheeks, he covered them with love bites and entered her from behind. Doggy style, as they called it in the mess, was one of his favourite positions, and it felt so good that he put his head back and shouted, "Wuff, wuff, wuff!" Meanwhile, Cassandra continued to howl.

Everything was so wet *down there* that he hardly knew that, after taking a little rest, he had re-entered her by the wrong portal, but she made no objection, just scrunched up her face (for it hurt) and screamed even louder. It was tight in there, and before he knew what he was doing, he felt he was going to come, but he had too far gone to exercise the self-control needed to pull out, and just let fly. It was only later that he realised he had gone in by the back door and that it didn't matter.

He was so exhausted by that wonderful session, that he fell asleep. It was late afternoon when he woke up, and his hangover had gone. He felt so mellow, and so well-disposed towards Cassandra, that he forgot about his card game at the mess, and spent the evening with her on the verandah, sipping gin and tonic, and looking forward to an early night.

Cassandra was delighted. She really though he had reformed.

Cavalry Sabres

There was a sudden commotion at Dale Hall when its master arrived unexpectedly. Everyone had thought he was in London, and he had sent no word, so no preparations had been made.

"I'm sorry, Your Grace," said his Major Domo, "but everything is under dust sheets."

"That's not your fault, Parkin. I decided to come at short notice."

"Is Benson with you?"

"I have sad news about Benson. He died in London and was buried there. But it is my intention to hold a memorial service for him at St Peter's on Friday. Please announce this to the staff. In the meantime, I want you to take over his duties as my manservant."

Parkin bowed.

"It will be an honour, Your Grace."

That evening, the duke might have been seen wandering around the further regions of St Peter's churchyard. It was dark. The skyline was a silhouette of the churchyard elms against a blue-black background sprinkled with stars. There was no moon. The duke paused at an unmarked grave, said a prayer, then said out loud, in a low voice, "Thank you, Benson, my friend. You saved my life. You deserve better than this lonely spot. However, I will place a memorial tablet in St Peter's, and will ensure that your aged mother is looked after. Rest in Peace."

There were two days before the memorial service, and in that time, the duke attended to a thousand and one domestic matters. There were many more he would have liked to have to have addressed – such as the matter of the new almshouse, but there simply wasn't enough time.

There was one matter, however, that he dared not neglect. He sent for his old fencing master and told him that he might have to fight a duel. The fencing master gave a grunt of disapproval, but knew that it was not his business to attempt talk his noble pupil out of it. just to help him in whatever way he could. His first question was: "Who with?"

"A former officer of Hussars – Cawthorne."

"And you will be the challenger, I assume?"

"Yes."

The fencing master frowned.

"Then the choice of weapons will be his. He might choose pistols, but if I were him, I would choose swords. That would give him an undoubted advantage."

"That's why I sent for you."

"There's not much I can do to help you. The art of fencing is acquired by years of regular practice. Have you been keeping it up?"

"Until recently, yes."

The fencing master paced up and down as he turned the problem over in his mind. Then he went up to the duke, looked him straight in the eyes, and said, "Follow my advice and you might stand a chance. Cawthorpe will have been trained to use a sabre and will have trained in the Le Marchant method. It is a method designed for a cavalryman on horseback, and relies on the cut rather than the thrust. You have been taught according to the French School, which is more sophisticated, and is based on the thrust – so you must insist on using duelling swords: straight swords, with bell guards, like the ones we use."

"But if he has the choice of weapon…"

The fencing master cursed under his breath.

"Yes, of course. Well, we will practice with cavalry sabres. There is one other thing: you must wear a light coat of mail under your shirt. If you do, there is a good chance you will survive."

The duke was not sure whether he would, in fact, challenge Cawthorpe. He would attempt to get his divorce by legal means, but to do so, he would have to persuade Cawthorpe to come back to England, and somehow he couldn't see that happening.

IT WAS NOT DIFFICULT to find Cawthorpe's address. By the time of the duke's arrival, everybody on the island had heard the scandalous tale of 'Mr and Mrs Thorpe'.

He knocked on the door, presented his card and waited. After a few moments he was shown into the drawing room. Parkin, whom the duke had brought with him, waited in hall.

Cawthorpe had a resigned air about him as though he knew what to expect.

"Come for satisfaction, eh?"

"No, I came for a divorce."

Cawthorpe was more alarmed by this than if the duke had challenged him there and then. A divorce case would mean that his name would be dragged through the courts, which might threaten his chance of a commission – it would certainly delay it. But there was worse: when the divorce came through, Cassandra would be free to marry, and who would she want to marry? – him! It was impossible! Cawthorpe was not of an introspective nature; he preferred to take life as it came, but he had learned two things about himself over the years: one was that he military man by nature, and the other was that he was a confirmed bachelor. Linton's idea of a divorce would threaten both.

"I have the necessary papers to file a suit against you, but you must return to England to answer it."

"Return, be damned!" growled Cawthorpe.

"If it is a question of money, I will pay your expenses."

"You add insult to injury. I am not short of money."

The duke saw the drift of Cawthorpe's thinking, but he wasn't ready to give up yet.

"Perhaps you should discuss it with Lady Linton. I'm sure she will support the idea."

"Go to hell!" said Cawthorpe. "No doubt there is some other woman that you want to marry. Well, I will not be a pawn in your game. Leave this instant, or I will put a bullet through your brow."

He reached for one of the pistols that were displayed over the mantlepiece.

"What, and hang for murder? If we must fight, let us do it properly. Here is my gage."

His gage was not the steel gauntlet of his ancestors, but a beige kid glove. Nevertheless, it carried the same import.

At this moment, Cassandra appeared at the door.

"Robert!" she gasped. The maid said Lord Linton was here, but I didn't believe her. What does he want, Arthur?"

"Tell her," said Linton.

Cawthorpe tried to put it in the most negative light possible.

"He wants to marry some other doxy, so he wants a divorce."

"A divorce!" she exclaimed, grasping at once the implications. "Why, that would suit us perfectly! We could marry and become Mr and Mrs Cawthorpe. We might even be able to reinstate ourselves in Bermuda society."

"Don't you see? It's impossible!" snapped Cawthorpe. "It will mean disgrace – for all of us! In any case, there is a better way."

"What better way?"

"This!" he said, stopping to pick up Lord Linton's kid glove. "There! I have accepted his challenge!"

Cassandra gave a great gasp of panic.

"But how will that help?"

"Simple! I will kill him. My honour will be satisfied, and you will be free to marry."

"Don't be so sure of that!" said the duke, half to himself.

Cawthorpe laughed.

"I *am* sure, and do you know why? The choice of weapon is mine, and I choose swords, and to be precise: 1796 pattern cavalry sabres. I am an officer of Hussars – or was, until recently – and I am an expert in Le Marchant's sword exercises."

Cassandra cried out.

"No, not swords! My husband is an expert, too! He will kill you!"

Then she fainted.

THE DUEL TOOK PLACE at dawn next day on a deserted stretch of pink sand in a lonely cove on the North Shore. The rising sun cast long shadows over the beach, beautiful, in the mellow morning light, but with a sinister suggestion of death. Captain Harfield was Cawthorpe's second, and Parkin acted as the duke's second, though there was some concern about his lack of knowledge of the *Code Duello*. There was one other person, a surgeon, a necessary attendant at every duel.

The 1796 pattern cavalry sabre is arguably the finest sword ever made, and is a fearsome weapon. It has a pronounced curve to facilitate slashing attacks in cavalry action. The blade widens near the point, which gives it something of the balance of a meat cleaver, making slashes far more brutal than with a straight sword.

Captain Harfield held up a white handkerchief as a signal to get ready, along with the words, "En garde." The opponents made their bows, then crossed swords. Harfield said, "Allez," and the bout began.

Cawthorpe, with a confident sneer on his face, began with a typical Le Marchant diagonal slash, which was easy to parry. His riposte, with an upward slash along the same diagonal, was unexpected, and the duke had to take a step back to avoid it. Cawthorpe immediately took a step forward to keep his opponent under pressure, and made a horizontal slash at shoulder height, which would have taken the duke's head off, if it had connected, but the duke caught it with a vertical parry, and followed up with a quick lunge to the chest. The 1796 pattern cavalry sabre is not well suited to the lunge, and it was therefore unexpected. The point caught Cawthorpe in the middle of his chest, causing him to shout with pain, but there was no blood, because he, also, was wearing a mail shirt.

Cawthorpe took a few steps back, and looked at the duke with new respect. Then, with what can only be described as a war cry, he made a vicious attack with his sword whirling like a windmill in alternate diagonals. It was an attack that would have overwhelmed a less experienced opponent by its sheer speed and force, but there was nothing scientific about it, and all the duke had to do was to keep his head, and match each slash with a parry, while, at the same time, looking for an opening. It came, when Cawthorpe extended his left arm for balance. He would not have done this on a horse, because he would have been holding the reins, and it is strictly against the advice in Le Marchant's manual, because an extended arm can be lopped off as easily as the branch of a tree. The duke lunged at it, and a red streak appeared on his shirt.

At the same moment, a wild scream came from the side of the cove, and Cassandra ran out in great distress.

"You'll kill him!" she cried. "Stop!"

The men took no notice, for they could not afford to lose concentration for a second.

"First blood!" said the duke. "Concede."

"Stop!" yelled Cassandra, becoming hysterical. She was getting too close, so Harfield stepped in to move her away.

"*A l'outrance*," responded Cawthorpe, "it's the only way to settle it," and raised his sword for the downward slash that was designed to shiver helmets, but despite its force, a slight touch from the duke's blade was enough to deflect it to one side. The trouble with such a powerful blow is that, if it misses, it takes longer to recover your guard, and for a split second, Cawthorpe was wide open. The duke aimed another lunge, but this time for the armpit, which he knew would be unprotected.

Then everything seemed to happen in slow motion. The lunge was made, but suddenly, Cawthorpe's white shirt was replaced by something blue. The lunge landed in the middle of the blue and turned it red. Then an ear-piercing scream echoed round the cove, and the blue and red disappeared, and he was standing over the bleeding body of his wife.

Regardless of his opponent, he flung down his sword and knelt to help her.

"Surgeon!" he called, but even before the surgeon got there, he knew she was dead.

"What have I done!" he wailed.

Cawthorpe, his erstwhile enemy, was the first to reassure him.

"It's not your fault, Linton. She came between us. Harfield should have stopped her."

"I tried," said Harfield, "but look!"

He held up his hand and showed a bloody patch where she had bit him in her struggle to get free.

"I killed her," sobbed Linton.

"It was an accident," insisted Cawthorpe.

"Yes, but it was my blade that pierced her heart, and I am the one who promised before God to love and protect her!"

Captain Harfield, in his role as second, was more concerned about practical matters.

"Gentleman," he said, "duelling is not illegal in British law, though to kill in the course of a duel is judged as murder. However, neither of the combatants is harmed, and the death is the result of an unfortunate accident. I propose that we present it as such to the authorities, with the agreement of the good doctor, here. Shall we agree that we going for a *pique-nique* on the beach and that the countess unfortunately fell from the cliff. To do that is not to distort the facts of the case, for it was indeed an accident, but it will prevent any scandal which would certainly arise if all the facts were known."

There was some brief discussion of the proposal, but as no viable alternative was suggested, it was agreed unanimously.

AFTER THE FUNERAL, Linton and Cawthorpe met at Britney. The two enemies were almost friends now, brought together by the terrible accident on the North Shore.

"You're taking it very hard, Linton, if I may say so," said Cawthorpe.

"Because it was my sword that took her life," said the duke gloomily.

"It was her impetuosity that took her life. What! Stop a sword fight with anything less than pistols!"

"Impetuosity? It was love – for you, I am sorry to say. If she had given a fraction of that love to me, we might have been living happily together in Dale Hall at this very moment."

"Don't blame yourself," said Cawthorpe, "or me, for that matter. She had an impossible dream of perfect love. She didn't find it with you, and she didn't find it with me, either – what you saw in the cove was not love, so much as desperation."

Cawthorpe then went on to narrate the gradual breakdown of their relationship in the last few months, and its patching up on the basis of a lie. When his story was over, he sighed, shook his head, and knocked off a glass of claret in one gulp.

Then an new idea occurred to him.

"But, perhaps – forgive me if presume – perhaps there is a positive side. Perhaps the reason you sought a divorce is because there *is* someone else, and you are now free to marry that person."

The duke shook his head vigorously.

"Free, legally, perhaps, but morally, no. I could not face that – someone else – until I have expiated my terrible deed."

"What do you mean by 'expiate'?"

"I don't know."

There was a long silence while the duke consoled himself with another glass of Claret. Then he said, "What about you?"

"Ha, that's easy. My old regiment has been deployed to Belgium. Old Boney is on the loose again and the allies are assembling their forces. I want to be a part of it. After that letter of recommendation to the colonel here, I'm sure they would take me back. Come to think of it, why don't you join me? What better expiation could there be than to risk your life in the service of your country?"

The Duchess of Richmond's Ball

Lord Linton was accepted into the 18th Hussars as a cornet, and like all junior officers had to learn drill with the troopers, but, as the former Romeo of the Road, he was skilled horseman, a crack shot, an expert swordsman, and in excellent shape physically, and he could soon keep up with the most experienced cavalrymen.

Cawthorpe had been offered a commission as a lieutenant, and so was only one rank above him, but he didn't mind that. He was delighted to be back in his old regiment and spending his time on marshal matters instead of trying to satisfy the follies and foibles of a woman.

The only fly in his ointment was having to take orders from Major Wilkinson, and you can be sure that that gentleman looked out for opportunities to give him extra duty.

The regiment was quartered in Brussels in preparation for an attack by Napoleon's *Armée du Nord*, but the attack was not expected for at least another week, and the Duke of Wellington's agents believed Napoleon would attack at Mons, which was a day's march south. In the meantime, there was the Duchess of Richmond's ball to look forward to.

The ball was held at the Duke of Richmond's house in the Rue des Cendres, and the duchess had done everything to make it the most talked-about ball of the season. The ballroom, a former carriage-house, had been refurbished especially, with garlands of flowers wrapped around the pillars, hundreds of candles in golden candelabras, and ensigns of many regiments ranged around the room to add a marshal note to the decoration. Best of all, she had managed to persuade the colonel of the Gordon Highlanders to provide a display of Scottish sword dancing.

As early as 10 o'clock the carriages began to arrive, and by the time Linton and Cawthorpe made their appearance, the Rue des Cendres was blocked with coaches and carriages.

As they eased their way through the crowded entrance hall, the skirl of bagpipes began, and they found that the dance floor had been cleared for the sword dance. Four sergeants, in full dress uniform, including kilts, laid their swords in an x-pattern on the floor, and began to dance in stockinged feet.

"One day I'll see it," said Cawthorpe.

"What" said Linton.

"Blood! One false move and his feet will be cut to ribbons. Those are service swords, you know – sharp as a razor!"

After the sword dance, the orchestra played a waltz, and Cawthorpe's attention turned to the ladies.

"I'll tell you what, Linton, all that fannying around in Bermuda made me hungry for a bit of army action, but after two months of it, I'm ready for a bit of... well, fanny."

The duke winced at Cawthorpe's casual tone, for the events in Bermuda had been the most harrowing of his life, but Cawthorpe failed to notice and continued in the same vein.

"And what better place to find it than this? A uniform is magnet for the fair sex at any time, but with a battle in prospect we'll be fighting them off. The thought that we might be killed will go to their sentimental little hearts, and they'll let us have anything we ask for."

But Linton wasn't listening. He was talking to the Duke of Richmond who had seen him come in. Dukes are a rare breed, so it is not surprising that they all knew each other.

"Good to see you in uniform, Linton," said the duke, magnificent in his general's uniform. "Sorry to hear about that accident. Please accept my condolences."

Linton made a slight bow, and quickly changed the subject.

"You wife has done us proud, Lennox."

"Indeed, yes. Wellington will be here later. You know him, of course."

"I know who he is, but I don't think I have ever spoken to him."

"Then I will introduce you, but excuse me, I must circulate."

Linton bowed again, and looked round for Cawthorpe. But he had already made his move, and was to be seen whirling round the dance floor with a young lady in a pink merino gown and a turban hat with high feathers. She was looking up at him admiringly, and already they were deep in conversation. But if Linton thought that it was affairs of the heart they were talking about, he was wrong; she was asking him about the French army.

"Are the rumours true?"

"Yes they are," replied Cawthorpe, airily. "We're off tomorrow. Nobody knows where, officially, but I have heard it whispered that it will be Mons."

"Tomorrow!" she gasped.

"Yes – and I dare say that some of us won't come back," said Cawthorpe, beginning his planned manipulation of her emotions.

"Oh, Arthur! Just as we were getting to know each other."

They got to know each other even better in the next two hours, because it seemed that the usual protocol of not monopolising a partner did not apply. Of course it didn't! Here were husbands, wives, young men and their fiancées, young couples still at the courtship stage, and indeed, couples like Cawthorpe and Sarah, and it seemed the most natural thing in the world that they wanted to spend the evening together.

Linton had no intention of dancing, but he found himself in conversation with Lady Frances Webster, who was reputed to be the mistress of both Lord Byron and the Duke of Wellington, and was so fascinated by her, that when the next waltz began, he asked her to dance.

She accepted graciously, but warned him about her pregnancy, "I may be a little awkward, as my baby bump is beginning to show."

"I will be gentle with you," said Lord Linton.

He led her onto the floor and they started to dance. She danced well, and her 'baby bump' seemed to make little difference to her agility.

"How Byron would have loved this!" she enthused, as she took in the scene: the decorations, the brilliant illumination, the dancers. "I shall describe it to him, and perhaps he will write a poem about it." (He did).

Her high spirits were such that the duke felt his spirits rising in sympathy. It was just what he needed after months of military endeavour, striving to prepare himself for the expiation that he so desperately desired.

"Will he write about the battle, too?"

"Perhaps. But someone else will have to describe that to him, for I have no intention of donning a hussar's uniform and dashing about in the mud all day!"

As the dance ended, a stir was taking place in the hall, and word was passed that the Duke of Wellington had arrived.

"Do excuse me," said Lady Frances, "but I have been waiting for him all evening."

No sooner had she left him than Cawthorpe appeared at his side and introduced his recent conquest.

"Miss Taylorson, allow me to introduce a good friend of mine and a fellow officer, Lord Linton, Duke of Wharfedale."

She made low courtesy (as is appropriate for a duke), which brought her feather perilously close to his face (though she didn't notice it). Then a Polka was announced, and she tugged at Cawthorpe's hand to lead him back onto the dance floor.

"I'm well away here!" he said, confidentially, before he followed her.

The Polka is an energetic dance, and soon they were both pouring with sweat. All the windows had been thrown open, but the press of people was so great, that there was more heat generated than if there had been a fire in the great fireplace.

"I'm hot!" declared Sarah, mopping her brow with a fine lace handkerchief.

"Yes, you are!" agreed Cawthorpe.

"I mean, it's hot in here!"

"Let me get you a fruit punch."

"No, I want to dance."

The Polka was followed by a slow waltz, which gave Cawthorpe the chance to 'move in for the kill'.

"It will be time for supper, soon," said Cawthorpe. "But I'm not hungry."

She gave him a sympathetic look, perhaps thinking that his fears for the battle had taken away his appetite.

"Not for food, anyway," he continued. "I'm hungry for love – for you!"

"Oh, Arthur!" she sighed.

"Let's find a place where we can be alone, so that we can – talk."

He led her from the dance floor to a store room nearby, which he had identified earlier as a suitable place, but he had only half opened the door when he heard sounds of heavy, rhythmic breathing, accompanied by moans and groans – somebody had beaten him to it. It was the same everywhere. Every bedroom was occupied, every store room, every cupboard that was large enough, contained a couple making love.

"You were right about it being hot in here!" said Cawthorpe, "but where can *we* go?"

"I know," said Sarah. "I'll have our coach sent round. We can drive around for a while while we – talk."

And what a conversation it was! – it was body talk of course: her ruby lips said, "Kiss me!" and he did. Her fulsome breasts said, "Suckle me!" That too. Her triangle of golden pubic hair said eloquently, "Come inside!" His body answered, standing to attention, and after knocking at the door a few times, he went inside – but it was not indecision that made him go in and out, in and out, but a desire to please. Her legs wrapped herself round his body and said, "Come inside," with a different meaning this time, so he did and showered her with his – appreciation.

Now his body said, "I hope you don't mind if I slip out," and by this time they had gone round the block and were back in the Rue des Cendres. Her tongue, which she had just put in his mouth, said, "Again!" So he knocked on the carriage roof and called, "Drive on!" but a certain limp member said, "I'm resting." Sarah's lips did their best to revive the limp member and prepare it for action, and when it felt the back of her throat, it replied, "I'm ready!"

Sarah turned over and sprawled over the seat, which would have presented a fine sight if there had been more light, for they were no in the country, and it was dark. So touch had to do the work of sight, and those two creamy mounds said eloquently, "Come inside!" though a little wriggle added, "but not by the backdoor."

The rocking and rolling of the carriage over the rutted country roads would have been enough in itself to give pleasure, but their bodies were deep in the to and fro of a conversation that had more than twice the energy. Her wetness said, "More! Harder! Deeper," and the slapping of his testicles on her pubes said, "Take this, and that, and that!"

It was not long before Cawthorpe, too, lay sprawled on a seat, utterly spent – no, not quite utterly. A little tingle down below said, "You could manage five shots in a night when you were 25, so surely you can manage another tonight!"

And that was how he lost track of time.

MEANWHILE, MOST OF the guests had gone to the dining room for supper. The Duke of Wellington was escorting the Duchess of Richmond and Lady Greville out of the ballroom, when a late arrival, Lieutenant Webster, hurried up to him and handed him a piece of paper. The duke slipped the paper into his pocket without reading it and asked Webster to join them.

While the first course was being served, the duke took out the paper and read it. He looked incredulous for an instant but quickly mastered his anxiety and resumed an air of nonchalance – which he considered important to maintain good morale. He finished his supper, playing the same, relaxed, unconcerned part throughout, then turned to Richmond and said, "I think it is time for me to go to bed. By the way, have you a good map in the house?"

Richmond said that he had and led him to his study. Wellington looked at the map with Webster's information in mind: the French had attacked at Quatre Bras, a crossroad to the south of Brussels. That meant that the enemy was much nearer than he had thought.

"Napoleon has humbugged me by God!" he exclaimed with horror. "He has gained 24 hours' march on me!"

"What do you intend to do?" said Richmond.

Wellington studied the map again, then placed his finger on a village nearer to Brussels with the name of Waterloo.

"I shall have to fight him *here*. I will give the order that ever man is to rejoin his regiment by three o' clock!"

The word was passed quickly, and the most famous ball in history came to a sudden and dramatic end. There was many a tearful parting, many a lingering kiss with the thought that it might be the last in this world, many a broken heart. The urgency was so great, that some officers felt that they dared not waste time changing into their uniforms, and fought at Quatre Bras in their evening dress.

WHEN CAWTHORPE AND Sarah got back to the Rue des Cendres, the house was practically deserted. There was hardly a man present, and many of the women had gone home. Only a few lingered with the duchess who was sobbing her heart out, partly because of the ruin of her ball, which should have gone on till dawn, and partly in fear for her husband's life.

"Ecod! I've missed it!" cried Cawthorpe, and without a word to Sarah, he ran to the stables calling for a horse.

He reached Quatre Bras just as the battle was ending.

Waterloo

Cawthorpe found that he was the laughing stock of his regiment, and the butt of such quips as: "Here he is! The boudoir warrior!" "He'd rather stick his sabre in a doxy than a French dragoon!" "Well, a bed is a softer battlefield!" "I'll bet she won and left his sabre limp!" so he made certain that he was present and correct at Waterloo, two days later.

He was eager to make up for his dereliction of duty on Friday, so he was frustrated to find that the 18th Hussars were to be held in reserve. Worse, Major Wilkinson had positioned him in the rearmost rank, so when they did go into action, he would be among the last to go.

The morning passed in preparation, Wellington was behind the small farmhouse of La Haye, and Napoleon, across the valley, was plotting his strategy in another farm house, La Belle Alliance. The key to Wellington's position Was Hougoumont – an acquisition which he saw as the ace in his pack. It was a large, walled farmhouse in the epicentre of the battlefield, and he knew that, if he could control that, he could control the battle.

Napoleon also realised its significance and made it the focus of his first attack, led by his 2nd Cavalry Corps, but the Coldstream Guards held them back with a rain of lead from their Brown Bess muskets, fired from loopholes knocked through the walls of the farm. The 2nd Corps fell back, but another wave of cavalry replaced them, and another and another. But they failed to take the farm.

Cawthorpe could hear everything, but see nothing, because it was a key point of Wellington's tactics to keep his reserves out of sight. He kept standing up in his stirrups (not that it made any difference) and saying, "What's happening? Why doesn't he send us in?"

Jenkins, who was just in front of him, said, "They say they're fighting over a farm halfway down the hill."

"A farm! What good is that? He should send in the cavalry!"

Nearby, Lord Linton listened to the thunder and lightening of war with exultation. His hour was come, and God would decide whether death or injury would be his expiation.

At about 11 o'clock Napoleon's *Grand Batterie* of 80 guns began a general bombardment, and at last, Cawthorpe felt he was part of things, for many of the balls came over the crest of the hill and fell on the reserves. The order for the infantrymen was: "Lie down!" and beside him a nervous cornet jumped off his horse to do the same.

"Not us, Spence – we must stand the shot!" barked Cawthorpe. "Now, mount!"

The poor cornet, who was just fifteen, still bobbed and ducked in the saddle.

"Keep still, Spence! An officer must show indifference. If it looks as though you are panicking, the men will panic, too!"

Just then a ball took Spence's leg off and he fell from his horse screaming. He was one of many casualties of the bombardment.

"Send for the medical officer!" called Cawthorpe, then added under his breath. "Why doesn't he give the order to attack? We're dying like flies here – and for nothing!"

Then suddenly the bombardment stopped.

"What's happening?" called Cawthorpe.

"Boney's probably making another attack," said Jenkins.

And he was right. Napoleon had sent his 1st Corps of Infantry in a huge column to march up the hill directly at Wellington's front line. They came on relentlessly, and as men fell, others took their place. There seemed to be no stopping them. The French *45e Ligne* were the first to reach the summit, and drove the British back with a great cheer. Napoleon was winning the Battle of Waterloo.

Wellington ordered a counter attack by his heavy cavalry, the Life Guards, the Royal Horse Guards, the King's Dragoon Guards, and others, but the regiment that made the biggest difference was the Scots Greys. They crashed into the French column and mowed men down like wheat. The *45e Ligne* faltered and the tide turned against the French.

"What's happening now?" said Cawthorpe.

"Wellington's deployed the heavy cavalry."

"Come on, then, we should charge!" and with these words he began to edge his horse forward.

"Halt, I say!" barked Wilkinson. "Wait for the word of command!"

Damn that man! thought Cawthorpe. If Boney wins, it will be his fault!"

As a response to the British heavy cavalry, General Ney ordered most of the French cavalry into action: 5,800 swords, in total, consisting of the cavalry corps of cuirassiers and the light cavalry division of the Imperial Guard. The Scots Greys were spent and could do nothing to stop them. This was the kind of attack that Wellington's tactic of infantry squares was designed to counter.

The order was passed: "Fix bayonets, form squares and stand firm!"

The colonel of the 18th Hussars knew that their moment was coming, and passed the word: "Ready!"

Cawthorpe drew his sword, settled himself firmly in his seat, and watched the horizon. But there was still a while to wait.

The French cavalry could achieve nothing against the squares, for a horse will not willingly impale itself on a bayonet. The horses would balk and rear when they approached the square, and the first rank could shoot horse or rider, then retire to the fourth rank to reload.

Seeing this, Napoleon recalled the cavalry, and played his ace – the Imperial Guard. Their reputation alone was as good as a 100 cannon, and the British soldiers, and perhaps some of their officers, quailed at the sight of the mighty column that marched towards them.

Wellington assessed the situation. His heavy cavalry were spent, though his infantry still held the ridge. It was time to send in the reserves, and the order was passed.

The colonel of the 18th Hussars ordered the bugler to sound the trot. They were off! Cawthorpe gave a grim smile. 'Boudoir warrior' indeed! He would show them! Linton also smiled, though his smile had an otherworldly quality, like that of a martyr entering the Roman amphitheatre, for he believed that he was on his way to expiate that terrible deed.

The 18th trotted over the crest, then, seeing the Imperial Guard marching up the hill, the colonel shouted, "Charge!" and a bugle call repeated the order. This was how Cawthorpe described it later (somewhat boastfully it must be admitted):

"Ah! there is nothing like a cavalry charge! the excitement of speed, the wind in your hair, the union between man and horse – the sheer exhilaration of it! In no time at all we were upon the enemy – and what an enemy! Chasseurs of the Old Guard – Napoleon's elite troops! I aimed for the shining breastplate of a magnificently mustachioed guardsman, but my sabre snapped on impact with his armour. The guardsman slashed at me with his French longsword, but I parried his blow with the hilt of my broken sabre. Unfortunately, his blade was deflected down and into my leg – though I didn't feel it at the time – and that was how I got my wound. With his guard down, he was an easy target, and I pushed my broken blade into his face. He fell, screaming, from his mount. Whether I killed him or not, I have no idea, because another guardsman was upon me. I thought that would be my end, because I had nothing but a broken fragment of blade, but suddenly he wheeled his horse and fled."

But Lord Linton had the worse of it. He hacked his way through the pack, slashing blindly to left and to right in a way that would have made his fencing master frown. He realised then why the Le Marchant school of fencing emphasised the slashing stroke: it is the natural reaction in close combat. Fortunately, he had trained in it with his fencing master, and when training as cornet, and his 1796 pattern cavalry sabre was designed for it, and now it seemed that every opponent fell back before him.

Then all at once he was through the pack and alone, except for a few other hussars like himself, who had somehow got ahead of the others. He was dangerously exposed, and his horse was blown. He turned around to ride back to his regiment, but before he could spur his horse forward, a sniper's ball slammed into his right arm and knocked him off his horse. He fell heavily, lost his busby, hit his head on something hard and blacked out. It's just as well that he did, because the French soldiers, who were milling about him in a disorganised retreat, took him for dead, and left him alone.

When he came round it was dark. The battlefield was deserted, but there was an eerie whining sound in the air. He couldn't identify it at first, but then he realised it was the groans of the hundreds of wounded and dying. He was conscious of a searing pain in his right elbow, and an unbearable thirst. But above all, he was cold, freezing cold. He pulled his Hussar's pelisse over him, but it was a small garment, and made little difference. Then he noticed that, lying beside him was a dead Frenchman wearing a heavy greatcoat. That was just what he needed, and with a superhuman effort, he managed to get him out of it. He searched the body in the hope of finding a water bottle, but there was nothing, so he wrapped himself in the greatcoat and, after all that effort, passed out again.

He woke up to find himself in an old barn with several other wounded soldiers. A medical orderly came up to him and removed the greatcoat, then shouted in surprise: "Sacre blue! Il est anglais!"

He was French, and had seen his Hussar's uniform. Linton guessed that he must have been taken from the battlefield by someone, probably Belgian pillagers, who thought he was French and had tried to save his life. No doubt his Hussar's uniform had helped. They would surely have seen it under the greatcoat, which was only draped over him, not worn and buttoned, but because his uniform was blue, it was not such an obvious giveaway as the bright red worn by most British soldiers.

The medical orderly shouted for a guard, and Linton found himself a prisoner of war. Nevertheless, the French are a civilised nation (some say the most civilised on earth) and his treatment continued. The orderly explained that he would have to amputate the arm as the joint was smashed, and it must be done immediately before infection set in. Linton, who spoke a little French, agreed, and braced himself for the operation. He was almost glad of it. This was a just expiation indeed! God had ruled that he should lose the arm which had killed his wife, but had spared his life, so he believed, so that he could do good to the people of Wharfedale.

The orderly made his preparations, washed the arm, placed a tourniquet around the upper arm, and inserted the knife. Linton passed out.

Fred Figgit Again

In the meantime, Fred Figget was fighting his own battle; the battle to win Dolly. He knew that a frontal attack would be routed at once, and decided on a tactical approach. He bought a gig of light, modern construction, and had it painted yellow. It was the nearest a man in his condition of life could come to a curricle, and while a sporting aristocrat might have sneered at it, it caused quite a stir amongst the farmers' daughters of the Dale.

One morning, he drove it into Bramham Farm. Dolly and Molly were at the pump scrubbing milk churns. Dolly's mane of red-gold hair hung untidily over her face, which was flushed with the effort of working the pump. She was wearing a grey calico gown with a soiled apron over it, and nothing at all on her feet. She stood up, swept back her hair, and regarded her visitor with surprise. She felt that she looked a fright, though in fact, the wildness of her hair and her heightened colour made her look better than ever.

"Ah wa' just passin'," said Fred, as casually as he could.

The two milkmaids smiled at each other. It was a poor excuse, because no road 'passed' the farm, you had to ride directly towards it for at least a mile if you wanted to get there – unless you struggled through Bramham wood from the turnpike road.

It seemed to Fred that the tables had been turned since their last meeting. Here he was perched on the seat of his new gig, in his new suit of York-tailored clothes, looking down at a mere milkmaid. How could he know that the mere milkmaid was promised to a duke?

He was tempted to say, "'Ow do yer like me new gig?" but he knew that it was more effective to let it speak for itself – and Dolly was not unimpressed. He had made something of himself since that naive proposal at the Race Week Barn Dance, and the months in-between when he had retired to lick his wounds. He would certainly make an excellent husband for the daughter of one of the duke's wealthier tenants.

"'Ow do yer like it 'ere?" he said, hoping that she didn't like it at all, and that she would see him as a chance to get out of it.

"Well enough," she said.

"I looks like 'ard work."

"It is, but ah don't mind. Pa made me work, yer know."

"Yeah, but not rough work like yer doin' now."

There was no answer to this, so she said instead, "Will yer step inside an' tek summat? Is that all reet, Molly?"

"Aye, but don't be long. This lot's got ter be done afore milkin' time."

Fred got down from his gig and she led him into the parlour, Then she went to the kitchen and called, "Aunt, Fred's 'ere!"

"Well ah'll go to t' foot o' our stairs!" said Aunt Dalton, wiping her hands on her apron in a panic. "Ah nivver thought we'd see 'im again after t' way you treated 'im!"

"Shush, aunt! 'Ee'll 'ear yer."

Aunt Dalton took off her apron and went to greet the visitor.

"Yer'll tek a cup o' tea – or per'aps yer'd prefer a tankard o' ale."

Fred preferred the ale, but he thought that Dolly would think tea more gentlemanly.

"Tea, please," he said.

Then Dolly played her masterstroke.

"Ah'll leave you two ter chat while ah 'elp Molly ter finish t' churns."

Fred looked horrified at being left with her aunt – it was not she that he wanted to talk to!

Molly'll finish that," said Aunt Dalton.

"There's too many for 'er to do by 'ersel', an' them churns 'ave to be done afore milkin' time."

With those words she hurried out before either of them tried again to detain her. She didn't return to the pump, though. Instead, she went through the little wicket gate at the back of the farm, and hid herself in Bramham wood until Fred had gone.

It wasn't long before she saw the yellow gig driving away from the farm. It wasn't that her aunt's conversation was boring (though it was), but that he had got the message – for now, at any rate.

Molly picked up the subject as soon as Dolly returned to the pump.

"Ah see 'ee's after yer again."

"Well, I don't want 'im."

"Why not? 'Ee's everythin' a man should be. Did yer see 'is gig, an' them nice clothes 'ee was wearin'."

"You can 'ave 'im, then."
"But it's you 'ee wants."
Dolly laughed.
"Leave Fred Figgit ter me, ah'll fix it for yer!"

IT WAS A SOLEMN DAY when the message came to Dale House that Lord Linton was "Missing, presumed dead." Stubham, his agent, called Midgley, the family lawyer, and consulted him about what should be done. Midgley frowned over the word "presumed".

"I'm afraid it means that the Wharfedale Estate will be *in limbo* for a long while. You see, a person has to be missing for seven years before I can apply to the court for a legal declaration that they are, to all intents and purposes, dead. Then the normal Probate and Estate Administration procedures can be followed."

It was a blow for all the people of Wharfedale – put simply, nothing would get done, there would be no development, only essential repairs would be made, and the new almshouse would not be built. But it was an even bigger blow to a certain person at Bramham Farm.

Dolly knew that Robert had gone to fight in France. He had not thought it proper to write to her while his wife was still alive, but soon after her death, he wrote to her telling her the whole story, and trying to explain how he felt. He wrote again soon after explaining that he felt he must go to France to try to expiate his deed.

She understood his feelings and thought they did him credit, and had no doubt that he would return to her when the war was over – not just return to her as a secret lover in a haystack, but to ask her to be his wife.

When she heard the news that he was missing, she couldn't believe it at first, and felt certain that he would turn up any day. She kept asking about him, and had it not been for the fact that others were asking about him too, her aunt would have been suspicious.

As the months went by the people of Wharfedale began to accept they had lost their duke, and settled down to wait for the expiry of the seven years that would bring them a new duke – Linton's distant cousin from over the Pennines. But Dolly's faith never faltered. She was sure that he was alive somewhere in France, and even toyed with plans to go and look for him. If she had done so, she would have found herself in good company, for many were the wives and lovers who went to look for their missing loved ones.

FRED REGROUPED HIS forces and decided on another assault. He was determined that, this time, he would not be fobbed off. He would get her alone, put the question to her and demand a straight answer. Surely by now she realised what was in her best interests.

So the yellow gig was once more spotted at the far end of the road to Bramham farm. Molly rushed into the cow byre with the news.

"'Ee's comin!"

"Who?" said Dolly, looking up quickly, thinking Molly was referring to the duke.

"Fred."

"Oh, Fred."

"Well, what are yer goin' ter do?"

Dolly remembered her promise to get Fred for Molly.

"Get down 'ere wi' me an' listen."

Dolly was milking a cow, so Molly took a three-legged stool and sat down to milk the cow next to her.

"Nah undo some laces," she said, pointed to the laces on the bosom of her gown.

"More!"

She undid them all so that when she leaned forward practically the whole of her breasts could be seen, just the two coral tips managing to stay inside.

"That's good. Them's yer best feature. The lads don't call yer 'Milkjugs' fer nowt."

"Ah thought they called me that cos ah'm a milkmaid," replied Molly, in all innocence.

"Yeah, a milkmaid wi' big jugs. Anyhow, mek sure 'ee gets a good look."

A moment later Fred rolled into the farmyard. He made an enquiry at the house and was directed to the cow byre. A moment later, he stood over them, looking very gentlemanly in his York-tailored clothes.

"'Ello, Dolly. 'Ello, Molly," he began.

"'Ello, Fred," they chorused.

Molly bent down to her task again, and her breasts bulged out. Indeed, it was a close call whether Molly or the cow had the most ample udders (in proportion to their size, of course). Fred's eyes bulged too, for a moment, and then he remembered his mission.

"Now, Dolly, ah'll not beat about t' bush, ah want a word wi' yer in private."

"Can't yer see ah'm busy," said Dolly.

"It'll not tek a moment. Ah think yer know what it's abaht."

Dolly seemed to think about it for a while, and all that could be heard was the squirt, squirt of milk into the pails. Fred gazed at the two sets of udders again and no doubt dreamed of going on a milk diet.

At last Dolly said, "Well, Fred, if yer want ter speak ter me in private, come back after dinner – let's say nine – an' meet me at the wicket gate to t' woods."

Fred thought it sounded promising – a night-time assignation in a private place – it meant a kiss at least, and perhaps more.

"All reet, then," he said, "but no games like last time. If yer not there, ah shall call at t' 'ouse, an' drag yer out!"

It was said in a joking manner, but she knew he was in deadly earnest.

"Yer'll not be disappointed, Fred," she said with a warm smile to him, and a wink to Molly.

He seemed satisfied, made his farewells, climbed into his gig and rode off.

"Ah thought 'is eyes were goin' ter pop aht!" laughed Dolly.

"Well, ah nearly did!" said Molly, lacing up her gown. "T' cows'll be after milkin' me if ah'm not careful!"

They had a good laugh at this idea, then Molly said, "But 'ow's that goin' ter 'elp me get 'im?"

Dolly put her head close to Molly's and whispered her plan.

FRED HAD BEEN WAITING anxiously by the wicket gate since eight. It was black as pitch in the woods, though a half moon cast a pale silvery light over the open fields. A few hundred yards away stood the house with a dim light in a back window, which he knew was the kitchen. He paced up and down, touching his gold repeater every few minutes to check the time.

"Women!" he thought. "What a lot o' trouble they put a man to! Why, wi' all the runaround that Dolly 'as put me to ah could 'a' gone all t' way ter China to sell 'em Wharfedale sickles!"

The thought of a Wharfedale sickle in the hands of a coolie in a conical cap made him feel a burst of pride – he was worth something, after all, and the girl should be grateful.

But here she was! A cloaked and hooded figure emerged from the kitchen door and tripped across the field. Of course, she was hurrying so as not to be seen – but she seemed eager enough.

A moment later she was in his arms.

"Dolly!" he sighed. "Ah knew yer'd come! All t' lasses 'ave ter play 'ard ter get, but a man like me likes 'is cards on t' table. Nah then, will yer marry me?"

She answered with a kiss, a passionate kiss such as he had never received in all his born days. It was a hot, wet kiss, that went all over his face, and into his mouth, with her tongue.

"Dolly!" he sighed, and held her closer. But something was not quite right. There was a fullness down there that did match the shape in his memory. He put his hand up to check, and found a fulsome breast.

"You're not Dolly!" he exclaimed, pulling away.

But Molly, for Molly it was, put into action a little trick that she had practised with Dolly. She had laced up the front of her gown with a slip knot so that one pull of the lace would let everything hang free. She pulled it, and the magnificent udders flopped into his hands. He recognised her now, for his bulging eyes at their last meeting had imprinted them in his memory. How wonderful they were to feel! Soft, elastic, yet firm at the tips! But he had to kiss them! A voice inside his head said, "Stop! Dolly will find out! You will lose her forever!" But his lips had a will of their own, and once he started suckling he had to keep going.

"Oh Fred!" sighed Molly.

"Oh, Molly!" sighed Fred, though his words were muffled by a faceful of udder.

There were other slip knots in that gown, and Molly knew that it was time to pull them, and soon Fred found that he was in another bush, besides those in Bramham Wood. He had no idea what he was doing there, or even what he was supposed to do, but like the animals on the farm he was following his instinct.

Instinct led him to shed his clothes and mount her like the prize bull mounts the cow. Molly egged him on all the way, as Dolly had advised her, for it is no disgrace amongst Dalesfolk to sample the goods before marriage. For a woman, it is a way to make sure of getting her man – especially if she gets pregnant, and for a man it is a way of ensuring that his woman will be a good bedmate – and a fertile one.

Fred had never experienced an orgasm inside a woman before, and he was surprised that it was accompanied by a flash of light – except when he found out that the flash of light came from Dolly's lantern.

"Well, Fred Figgit!" she said, with mock indignation. "Ah thought yer was waitin' fer me!"

A One-Handed Farm Hand

Napoleon abdicated on the 22nd of June, and Lord Linton, along with other prisoners of war, was released. His arm had not healed properly as there was suppuration around the stump, so he was transferred to St John's Hospital in Brussels. During his time in the hospital he wrote several letters to his Agent and to Dolly, though in a clumsy, left-handed scrawl.

It was late September before he was pronounced fit to travel. He was eager to be off, but wrote his last letter from Belgium before he began his journey. It was a letter to Dolly telling her of the probable time of his arrival. He had told her that he would come to Bramham Farm immediately, and that she was to wait for him there.

His time as an invalid had affected him badly. He was a shadow of his former self. He had had a second amputation, making his stump shorter, and had thus been laid in bed in one place or another for nearly three months. He had lost weight and muscle tone, and his skin was a pasty white. His features looked drawn and haggard, and he was unsteady on his feet. However, unlike many of the other casualties of war, he experienced none of the psychological problems of losing a limb. There were some, young men, especially, who could not bear the thought; who felt that they not whole men anymore, and who thought of suicide. This was particularly true of those who had lost a leg, or who had been blinded, but Linton felt that his disability was nothing less than an act of God – a just punishment for what that arm had done – and he felt cleansed and, strangely, whole.

He was repatriated with a group of convalescents from various regiments under the watchful eye and helpful hand of a medical orderly. They exchanged stories of their experiences at Waterloo: an officer of artillery whose cannon had exploded in his face, and left him blind and disfigured; a infantry officer whose leg had been taken off by a cannonball, and a lieutenant of dragoons whose right hand had been sliced off by a French sword. Sometimes they told tales of their experiences in the battle, sometimes they spoke of home, and sometimes they joked that, only together did they make one whole man. But there were times of silence when each was alone with his thoughts, wondering, no doubt, how he would get on in the life that awaited him.

It was a wonderful moment for all but one when they saw the white cliffs of Dover on the horizon. That one, who would never see anything, ever again, shed bitter tears because he was denied that beautiful sight – a bitter reminder of all the other things hew would never seen again: the setting sun, trees and flowers, and the faces of his loved ones.

They parted at Dover to go their different ways. Linton thought at first that he might stay for a few days, take gentle exercise, walk along the top of white cliffs and inhale lungfuls of sea air to build up his strength for the arduous 20-hour coach journey along the Great North Road. But he couldn't wait, so, weak as he was, he set out on his journey.

FRED KNEW THAT IT WAS all up with him and Dolly, and that there was nothing he could do or say to put matters on their old footing. But he was not displeased with his bargain. Molly was a fine woman, and he knew that she would make him a good wife (indeed, she demonstrated it on many subsequent trysts in those same woods). Being an honest Dalesman, and being caught with his trousers down, Fred did the right thing and proposed. A Christmas wedding was decided upon and the preparations began.

Dolly was almost jealous. There was no news from France, and it seemed more and more certain that her duke, her lord and lover, was dead – and Fred would have been an acceptable compromise. He was a good-natured soul who would have been easy to get along with on a day-to-day basis, and though very far from being a duke, was as good as any gentleman farmer.

She particularly liked the idea of a Christmas wedding, and often dreamed that it could be between her and her duke instead of Molly and Fred – it would be hard to get through their wedding without a tear, but she knew that she must steel herself to do it.

In the meantime there was work to keep her mind off things, and more of it than usual, because Molly, at Fred's request, had gone to live with her mother to prepare for the wedding.

One morning, she was in the byre milking the cows when she heard a voice behind her.

"D' ye know if t' mistress 'as any work fer a gen'ral farmhand?" said the voice, in a broad Daleish accent.

"Nay, it's a milkmaid we want," she said without looking round.

"Ah can turn me 'and to milkin', though ah've only one, mind."

One hand, and looking for work on a farm! How strange, thought Dolly turning round to look.

She saw what looked like an ordinary Dalesman in a rough cambric shirt with an old brown cloak thrown over it. He looked haggard and pale, and had not shaved for a day, but there was no mistaking those penetrating blue eyes.

"Robert!" she gasped, throwing herself into his arms. "I thought you were dead!"

He was aghast.

"Did you not get my letters?"

"No, nothing."

He shook his head.

"I should have realised. The aftermath of the war was chaotic. I expect they'll make there way here sooner or later."

"It's so good to see you!"

"You too!"

They kissed for a very long time, and would have continued kissing had not Aunt Dalton shouted from the front door, "Dolly, what on earth do yer think yer doin', kissin' that ragamuffin!"

"This is no ragamuffin, aunt, it's L..."

Before she could say 'Lord Linton' he put a hand over her mouth.

"Robin," he called to Aunt Dalton. "Robin Dale, and ah've just asked yer niece to marry me."

"No you haven't!" Dolly whispered.

"In effect," he whispered back.

"I don't want 'in effect' I want the proper words."

"Very well. Will you marry me?"

"That's better!"

Now it was the duke's turn to be pernickety.

"I don't want an evaluation of my question, I want a straight answer?"

"Are yer goin' ter stand there whisperin' all day?" protested Aunt Dalton.

"No," said Dolly.

"What!" exclaimed the duke, with mock horror.

"I mean, 'yes', to you," and kissed him to prove it.

"There yer go again," complained Aunt Dalton.

"It's all right, aunt, we're going to be married."

"And why are yer talkin' all lah-di-dah?"

"Because we're going to be married!" said the duke

"Oh, I forgot," he said, whispering again. "Let's keep our secret for a bit longer just for the fun of it."

Dolly laughed.

"What a wonderful idea!"

"Ah 'ope yer not laughin' at me!" said her aunt indignantly.

"No, aunt, we're laughin' cos we're going' ter be married."

"Humph! Well, ah'm not so sure abaht that. What's 'ee got ter offer yer? 'Ee's only a farm labourer – or was. It looks like 'ee's only got one arm."

"Ah wa' in't army at Waterloo. Ah've got prize money. Ah'm goin' ter lease me own little farm an' 'ire labourers. Ah can support 'er, dunna ye worrit thysen abaht that!"

Molly smiled at him, impressed by his command of the dialect – but Miss Dalton scowled.

"Well, we'll see what 'er feyther 'as to say abaht it!"

THE INTERVIEW WITH Dolly's 'feyther' was the weakest point of their plan, for the duke had often sat face to face with him in his office and rode side by side with him on his land. It seemed impossible that he would not recognise him. They decided to give it a try, however. His appearance had changed somewhat because of his illness, and common clothes and a Daleish accent helped the illusion. Perhaps the biggest help was Dolly's idea of not letting her father see him by daylight. They would go in the evening, when her father sat by the light of the fire and a single tallow candle for economy's sake.

Dalesman Dalton was, as Aunt Dalton had predicted, not pleased about it. But Dolly was stubborn, and when she showed him the 200 golden guineas that was his prize money from the war (and it really was: a cornet's prize money after Waterloo was exactly this amount), he was somewhat mollified. It was a great help that Fred Figget was now spoken for.

The next part of their plan was to persuade the Rev Hale to go along with it. He agreed, on certain conditions to ensure that their marriage complied with the law; in effect, the duke had to get a special license to get round the problem that the banns would be announced in the wrong name.

A Double Wedding

Fred and Molly planned to get married on Christmas Eve at 11 in the morning. Fred had had the idea of having a simple wedding breakfast at his family home, but saving the big celebration for the Christmas Dinner and Dance. It is true that last year's dinner and dance had been a bit of a let down, Stubham, the Land Agent, being reluctant to spend much of his absent master's guineas on what he described, rather unkindly, as a 'knees-up for nobodies', but Fred decided that it would be much better to supplement the dinner and dance fund than to pay for a separate celebration. That way, all the Wharfedale folk could be part of it.

Robin and Dolly agreed that it was an excellent idea, and that they would join in, too. Robin, of course, could afford to put half of his prize money into the dance, which meant that the 1815 Christmas Dinner and Dance would probably be the best ever in the history of the event.

Like Molly, Dolly went home to prepare for the wedding, and her aunt had another new milkmaid to find. Robin stayed on the farm to help, though with only one arm, there was not much he could do. He paid his way, however, and built up his strength with fresh air, good simple food, and occasional one-handed jobs, like working the pump while the new milkmaid washed the churns. But best of all were Dolly's visits, and they were worth getting his strength back for.

She would visit her aunt first, take tea, and bring her up to date with Wharfedale gossip, then she would say that she was going for a walk with Robin. However, they walked no further than the barn. The first time that he led her there, she said, "I thought you would prefer a comfortable bed after all you've been through."

He just laughed and tried to explain. "When you are on campaign you are grateful for a roof over your head. Before Waterloo, I had to sleep outside in the pouring rain. I've slept on floors, roofs, mud, rocks, and bug-infested hospital beds. Once I slept in a haystack, in a barn near Arras – I loved that, because it reminded me of you."

He picked her up, threw her into the hay and leapt on top of her, and in a moment they were rocking in their own private world – heaven in a haystack!

THE DOUBLE WEDDING took place at St Peter's Church. It was full to overflowing, as was to be expected with two groups of wedding guests. The pews in the side aisles were full, and the empty space at the back of the church around the font was packed with standing guests. Somebody, and it wasn't Frank, had paid for a magnificent display of flowers, with a floral arrangement at the end of each pew, and on the lectern and pulpit. The choir was four times larger than usual, and it was rumoured to have been supplemented by choristers from York Minster.

Frank and Robin waited in the front pew, along with their best men. Frank's best man was his work's manager, Mr Ackroyd, and Robin's best man was Matt, who looked very uncomfortable in the smartest suit of clothes he had ever worn in his life.

Robin wondered if Frank would recognise him, now that he was dressed in his best – but Frank had other things to think about, and his nerves made him fidget more than ever. He ran his hand through his hair, adjusted his cravat, toyed with his fobs, then went back to his hair again.

There was a hushed whispering in the congregation which the voluntary (played by the famous Matthew Camidge, the organist of York Minster) did little to hide. Then there was a sudden hush and a few excited whispers of, "They're here!" Everyone looked round, and there at the west door stood the two brides with their fathers. The organist played a fanfare, and Molly and her father walked down the aisle, to be welcomed by Rev Hale at the chancel steps. The organist modulated to another key, and played a different fanfare, and it was Dorothy's turn to walk down the aisle. The fanfare ended on a great, shuddering chord, and the two couples were ranged in a row before the vicar.

He read the prescribed ceremony from the Book of Common Prayer: an introductory homily, followed by the marriage vows. Frank and Molly took them first.

"Wilt thou, Frank, have this woman, Molly, to thy wedded wife, to live together after God's ordinance in the holy estate of Matrimony? Wilt thou love her, comfort her, honour, and keep her, in sickness and in health; and, forsaking all other, keep thee only unto her, so long as ye both shall live?"

"I will," ... and so on.

When the first couples' vows were complete, Rev Hale turned to Robin and Dolly with a conspiratorial wink.

"Wilt thou, Sir Robert, have this woman, Dorothy..."

There was a sudden uproar in the church, so much so, that Linton almost regretted his little joke. There were cries of: "Sir Robert!" "It can't be!" "Lord Linton!" "He's dead!" "The duke!" "He's missing!" "It is!" "He's here!"

Lord Linton turned to the congregation and bowed, but said nothing. Rev Hale raised his hands and said, "Dearly beloved brethren, never forget that we are in the House of God. It is indeed, His Grace, Lord Linton, whom I have the honour of joining in matrimony with Miss Dalton, so if you will permit me, I will continue."

He did, and the words that Dolly had so longed to hear were said at last:

"I now pronounce you man and wife."

Mr Camidge pulled out all the stops, no doubt wishing there were as many as on his organ in the minster, and played a thundering voluntary for their recessional, and soon they were out in the open air on a cold, but bright December morning, with everyone crowding around to shower them with rice and good wishes.

The couples went their separate ways for their wedding breakfast, Frank in his yellow gig, followed by a train of other carriages and carts, and Sir Robert and Dorothy in the duke's barouche, with the ducal arms of gryphons, martlets and chevrons much quartered, on each door. This was followed by carriages and carts, because Linton had decided not to invite his aristocratic friends and relatives in case it gave the game away and spoiled his surprise. Their time would come at the Christmas Ball, which, this year would have to be later than usual, on the 12th day of Christmas, January 6th.

THE CHRISTMAS DINNER and Dance began with toasts to the two happy couples and a few words from the principal actors. Precedence dictated that the duke should speak first, but he was adamant that the day had first belonged to Frank and Molly, and therefore Frank should speak first.

"Yer all know me, an' yer all know me story. All ah want to say is that God wanted me to 'ave Molly, an' ah'm glad ah've got 'er. A toast to the bride!"

The duke was next.

"Waterloo, and another event which I will not mention, nearly did for me. But God was good. He sent me back to Wharfedale, and he gave me Dorothy. Forgive me if I raise a toast with my left hand, but my right is 'missing, presumed dead'. A toast to the bride!"

Mr Ackroyd, as Frank's best man, spoke next.

"A best man usually tells a few jokes about t' groom, an ah could tell yer tales of what went on in Bramham Woods that would make yer 'air stand on end – or summat else mebbe! But the reverend is 'ere, so ah'll shut me gob afore ah say too much. A toast to the bride an' groom!"

Now it was Matt's turn. The only public speaking he had ever done in his life was to shout at a herd of cows, so he was trembling like a leaf when he stood up to speak.

"Well," he began awkwardly, "yer could 'a' knocked me dahn wi' a feather when me old pal Robin – a farm 'and like mesen – turned into a dook. It wa' like magic – an' whoever did it, ah wish they'd do it ter me."

He sat down, then stood up again suddenly and added, "Ooh ah, an' a toast ter t' bride an' groom!"

There was a roar of appreciation for this speech, and many voted it to be the best speech of the evening. Matt was suddenly famous, and best of all, a certain milkmaid by the name of Sally took notice.

Then the orchestra struck up – and what a sound! – this was not the old church band with their antiquated instruments, it was a professional chamber orchestra from York.

The duke had the honour to lead the dancing. Everybody expected that he would call for a waltz, but no, he called for one of the old country dances: Cuckolds-all-a-Row. Dolly laughed so much at his choice that she could hardly stand up straight, and because it is a very hard dance to do without a line of other couples – but, of course, they had done it before in this way. After the first set, the duke waved his arm to signal all the others to join in, and soon there was a line of 'husbands' and a line of 'wives', who would change partners in the course of the dance and make 'cuckolds'.

One country dance followed another in a headlong whirl of happiness until the church clock struck midnight and announced that it was time for supper. Another surprise awaited the revellers, for instead of the usual simple fare, there were delicacies fit for – well, a duke: turkey with stuffing, roast beef, ham, gravy, cranberry sauce, carrots, turnip and parsnips, and for dessert, pumpkin, apple pie, Christmas pudding and fruitcake. The good people of Wharfedale stuffed themselves as though *they* were the Christmas turkeys, some of them so much, that they couldn't get up again to dance.

Those that didn't eat too much, drank too much (and many did both), for there was every form of tipple to choose from. The speeches had been accompanied by Champagne (the first time that many Dalesfolk had tasted it), fruit punch, fortified with rum, was available all evening, along with the famous Wharfedale Ale – the preferred drink of the true Dalesman. Four types of wine were served with supper, and Brandy and a choice of liqueurs were available after.

The dance would go on until dawn, but when supper was over, the happy couples announced their intention of leaving for the final ceremonial of the day – the wedding night. As was customary, various lewd jokes accompanied their exit.

"There's plenty there for Fred ter fidget wi'!"

"Just pull it, Molly, like when yer milkin' a cow!"

"It won't matter abaht t' dook's missin' arm toneet, as long as 'ee's got a strong third leg!"

It wasn't far from the tithe barn to Dale Hall, but Sir Robert and Dorothy took the barouche for the sake of form. All the staff were ranged around the steps of the Gibbs portico, and they cheered as the duke carried his bride over the threshold. It wasn't easy, and the only way he could do it was to do what is known as a 'fireman's carry', that is to say, over the shoulder. It was quite amusing to see, as it looked as though he was one of his ancient Saxon ancestors abducting an indigenous Elmetian.

As they climbed the Grand Staircase, hand in hand, the duke said, "All this is yours, now. What do you think?"

"These stairs'll tek some cleanin'!" she said in the dialect.

The duke laughed, "You'll never have to clean again."

As they came to the door of the master bedroom, the duke paused and kissed her.

"I have a surprise for you, he said, "Cover your eyes."

She did, and he led her into the bedroom.

"Now you can look."

She took her hand away, and there before her was – a haystack.

"We've had our happiest times in a haystack," said the duke with a chuckle, "so I thought... but this is no time for words."

And with that, he picked her up as best as he could with his one arm, threw her into the haystack, and jumped in after her.

Epilogue

The Christmas Barn Dance marked the end of Dolly's old life, but she didn't really become Lady Dorothy until the Christmas Ball, which marked the beginning of her life as a duchess. In between were ten days when she was neither milkmaid nor duchess, but a lover in lovers' heaven – and if that heaven was a haystack, so much the better, because it was close to nature.

On the tenth day, the duke spoke seriously to her about her new life.

"Tomorrow you will meet all the great and good of Wharfedale. They know your background, so you don't have to pretend, but you must do your best to follow the expected conventions – and no more 'thees' and 'thous'. You are a lady now, and must speak like one."

He walked her round the ballroom, and explained how she must greet her guests, circulate among them, accept or refuse requests to dance, and generally how to be the perfect hostess. It was daunting, and for the first time, Dorothy wondered what she had let herself in for. She had always wanted to marry a duke, but she had not thought that a duchess would have to act like the manager of a London hotel.

She was very nervous when the guests started to arrive, and self-conscious about her words of greeting, her courtesies, and her small talk. She was conscious too, that these were dukes, earls, barons, landed gentry and the like, while she was nothing more than a Dalesman's daughter. Even the lower gentry, the clergymen, the doctors and the lawyers, overawed her. It did not help that several of their guests behaved condescendingly, or even snootily towards her. This was especially true of those who had been friends of the late duchess, and those who were, by nature, snobs.

But one man saved her by helping her to get it all in perspective: Major Cawthorpe (he had got his old rank back thanks to his exploits at Waterloo).

"Well, hello Dolly," he said, with an extravagant bow. "I never thought I'd see you standing beside old Linton, here."

Then he turned to Lord Linton.

"You're a lucky man, Linton, hey? Got a real woman at last – and about time too!"

Cawthorpe had that remarkable gift of ignoring convention, while never seeming to offend anybody. His secret, of course, was charm. Charm is a wonderful thing, but it is not without a degree of insincerity. Dorothy had something better than that: a kind heart, and it is that that won over the great and the good of Wharfedale. Slowly, it is true, and for the most snobbish, never, but as the years went by, they came to respect her. As for the Dalesfolk, they all loved her. After all, she was one of them, and she still spoke like them when she was among them, despite Robert's insistence that she should speak like a lady.

Like all marriages, it had its ups and downs: they were so different, after all, even though they were so close. During the 'downs' they would fight like cat and dog, until Sir Robert, realising that words could never get through, would drive her to the farm and throw her in a haystack. Even the smell of the hay brought back those wonderful early days – and, of course, that was only the beginning.

The ups were when the saw eye to eye on things, and that was often, especially in that matter which was closest to the duke's heart; the well being of the Dalesfolk. The new almshouse was finished, and the beggars swept up off the streets of Wetherby to live in relative luxury for their remaining years. Dorothy's part was to organise subscriptions, and this she did so well, that subscriptions brought in more money than even the Romeo of the Road had managed to extort in his heydey. The duke's next project was to organise a horse patrol to clear the highways of highwaymen once and for all, and his first success was to catch The Reverend Rogue, much to Mr Hale's satisfaction. He also built new cottages on the farms that he sublet to replace the leaking slums that most of the farmworkers had to live in. After that he planned to drain the wetlands in the Wharfe valley to make them productive, but that project had to wait for a while, because Dorothy presented him with a little project of her own: a son and heir. Sir Robert was in heaven, perhaps even a higher heaven than their haystack, because at last he had a son and heir, and the dukedom was secure for the next generation.

Did you love *The Duke and the Dalesman's Daughter*? Then you should read *Captain Cardew's Conquests* by Anne Harlowe!

Captain Cardew prefers balls at regional assemblies and small country houses because there he can meet the daughters of the lower class of gentry, who are impressed by his uniform and his rank, and are easily seduced. At one of these balls, at Hawtry Hall, he meets Millicent, a doctor's daughter, and Hannah, a clergyman's daughter, and seduces them both, one after the other. But, as he has found before, it is much easier to get into these affairs than to get out of them.

About the Author

Anne Harlowe was brought up in York, and was lucky enough to go to St Peter's School. The city, with its rich history and magnificent cathedral, has been an important influence in her life, and has inspired some of her best work. She read English at Leeds University, and did a master's degree dissertation entitled *Jane Austen's Heroines*. Her first attempt at writing for publication was to produce a study guide for *Pride and Prejudice*, but after about 20 pages she got distracted by writing a short story entitled *A Night at Pemberley*. This was submitted to a Fan Fiction website and was well-received, encouraging her to attempt further flights of Jane Austen-related fantasy, the most popular of which are *Darcy's Dark Secret* and *Poet of Pemberley*. Not content to hang on to the bonnet-strings of her favourite author, she began writing original works of Regency and Victorian romance, the most recent of which are *Captain Cardew's Conquests* and *The Romantic Adventures of a Between Maid*. The study guide is still unfinished.